T0338147

TEXTS & DOCUMENTS

A SERIES OF THE GETTY CENTER PUBLICATION PROGRAMS

The TEXTS & DOCUMENTS series offers to the student of art, architecture, and aesthetics neglected, forgotten, or unavailable writings in English translation.

Edited according to modern standards of scholarship and framed by critical introductions and commentaries, these volumes gradually mine the past centuries for studies that retain their significance in our understanding of art and of the issues surrounding its production, reception, and interpretation.

Eminent scholars guide the Getty Center for the History of Art and the Humanities in the selection and publication of TEXTS & DOCUMENTS. Each volume acquaints readers with the broader cultural conditions at the genesis of the text and equips them with the needed apparatus for its study. Over time the series will greatly expand our horizon and deepen our understanding of critical thinking on art.

Julia Bloomfield, Thomas F. Reese, Salvatore Settis, *Editors*
Kurt W. Forster, *Consultative Editor*, TEXTS & DOCUMENTS
THE GETTY CENTER PUBLICATION PROGRAMS

STYLE-ARCHITECTURE
AND BUILDING-ART

PUBLISHED BY THE GETTY CENTER
DISTRIBUTED BY THE UNIVERSITY OF CHICAGO PRESS

FOR THE HISTORY OF ART AND THE HUMANITIES

TEXTS & DOCUMENTS

STYLE-ARCHITECTURE AND BUILDING-ART:
TRANSFORMATIONS OF ARCHITECTURE IN THE NINETEENTH CENTURY AND ITS PRESENT CONDITION

HERMANN MUTHESIUS

INTRODUCTION AND TRANSLATION
BY STANFORD ANDERSON

THE GETTY CENTER PUBLICATION PROGRAMS
Julia Bloomfield, Thomas F. Reese, Salvatore Settis, *Editors*
Kurt W. Forster, *Consultative Editor*, TEXTS & DOCUMENTS

TEXTS & DOCUMENTS

Architecture
Harry F. Mallgrave, Editor

Style-Architecture and Building-Art:
Transformations of Architecture
in the Nineteenth Century
and Its Present Condition
Julius Posener, Editorial Consultant
Lynne Kostman, Managing Editor
Michelle Ghaffari, Manuscript Editor

Published by The Getty Center
for the History of Art and the Humanities,
Santa Monica, CA 90401-1455
© 1994 by The Getty Center
for the History of Art and the Humanities
All rights reserved. Published 1994
Printed in the United States of America

00 99 98 97 96 95 94   7 6 5 4 3 2 1

Permission to publish
an English translation of
Stilarchitektur und Baukunst
has been granted by Eckart Muthesius.

Library of Congress
Cataloging-in-Publication Data
is to be found on the last
printed page of this book.

CONTENTS

ACKNOWLEDGMENTS

I owe a special debt of gratitude to Harry Mallgrave for his thorough editing of both the translation of *Stilarchitektur und Baukunst* and my essay on that work. Professor Julius Posener of Berlin gave me welcome assurance through his appreciative reading of the essay. Dr. Hans-Joachim Hubrich of Everswinkel, Germany, kindly provided a copy of the second edition of *Stilarchitektur*, and my colleague Dr. Ákos Moravánszky always made himself available for consultation.

The library of the Getty Center for the History of Art and the Humanities, the Kunstbibliothek in Berlin, the Landesbibliothek in Karlsruhe, the Rotch Library of the Massachusetts Institute of Technology, and Professor Werner Oechslin of Einsiedeln, Switzerland, generously supplied copies of *Stilarchitektur* and other materials by or on Hermann Muthesius.

My assistants at MIT, Anne Simunovic and Samuel Isenstadt, endured every request. I am also grateful for the careful and solicitious efforts of those associated with the Getty Center: Julia Bloomfield, Michelle Ghaffari, Lynne Kostman, and Tyson Gaskill. My thanks also to the designer of this volume, Lorraine Wild.

—S. A.

1. HERMANN AND ANNA MUTHESIUS AT "THE PRIORY,"
HAMMERSMITH, ENGLAND, 1896. PHOTO: COLLECTION OF ECK-
ART MUTHESIUS.

INTRODUCTION

STANFORD ANDERSON

STYLE-ARCHITECTURE AND BUILDING-ART: REALIST ARCHITECTURE AS THE VEHICLE FOR A RENEWAL OF CULTURE

ALTHOUGH THE SMALL BOOK PRESENTED HERE, Hermann Muthesius's *Stilar-chitektur und Baukunst* (Style-architecture and building-art), 1902, was one of many turn-of-the-century programs calling for a renewal of culture, it deserves special attention for its effectiveness in architecture prior to the First World War.[1] In this book Muthesius established, early in the century and early in his career, the themes that would carry his advocacy of cultural renewal for a decade or more—themes that still deserve consideration. Even the Austrian Otto Wagner, one of the most prominent of the progressive architects of that moment, paid homage to this work by a younger German colleague. In 1896 Wagner published *Moderne Architektur*, his inaugural lecture as a professor at the Akademie der bildenden Künste in Vienna. Under the influence of *Stilarchitektur und Baukunst*, however, he changed the title of his fourth edition of 1914 to *Die Baukunst unserer Zeit* (The building-art of our time). Thus Wagner, despite a career notable for its devotion to a high architecture with evident references to past styles, found a polemical advantage, as did Muthesius, in preferring the German word *Baukunst* (building-art) to the Latin-based *Architektur*. Connected with this shifting perspective was the emphasis on the art of building "of our time." The three key words of Wagner's revised title sum up the major advocacy of Muthesius: a realistic approach to building in the service of new societal forces, an approach that Muthesius felt must leave stylistic precedent behind. Most particularly, classical paradigms, with their emphasis on ideal form, were to be abandoned in favor of a northern, process-oriented attitude toward building that was claimed to be manifested in the Gothic.

Born in 1861 in Gross-Neuhausen in Thuringia, Hermann Muthesius was the son of a mason and small building contractor.[2] A good student, he nevertheless trained as a mason before attending the Realgymnasium (higher secondary school) in Weimar. From 1881 to 1883 he studied art history and philosophy at the University of Berlin, followed by one year of military service. From 1883 to 1887 he studied architecture at the Technische Hochschule in Berlin and also worked for a period in the office of Paul Wallot, the famed architect of the German Reichstag.

Muthesius worked in Japan from 1887 to 1891 supervising contracts for the architectural firm of Ende and Böckmann. After this he returned to Germany and took state examinations. He then entered the Prussian Ministry of Public Works. In 1895 a state stipendium allowed him to make a study trip to Italy, which resulted in his first book, *Italienische Reise-Eindrücke* (Italian travel impressions), 1898.[3] At this point Muthesius already denied that contemporary artistic production stemmed from either the continual adoption of past styles or the invention of a new style. While respecting Italian art, he rejected its claim to universality and insisted that German architecture had to be built on a healthy, indigenous artistic tradition— though the periods he risked mentioning as still capable of allowing independent development were the Early Christian, Romanesque, and German Renaissance.

In 1896 Muthesius renewed his work at the ministry and also married Anna Trippenbach, a concert singer. In October of that year he was commissioned by the kaiser as cultural and technical attaché to the German Embassy in London (fig. 1). He was to report on British art, architecture, and technical achievements. In the course of his assignment, he developed an exceptional expertise on English crafts and architecture, which resulted in three major publications and simultaneously laid the ground for his own polemical positions on contemporary culture and architecture, as exemplified in the translation presented in this volume.[4]

The first of Muthesius's books on English architecture, *Die englische Baukunst der Gegenwart* (Contemporary English architecture), was an extraordinary folio on governmental, institutional, and commercial buildings of all types; it included as well a section on domestic architecture, which focused on larger urban houses and housing. Following an informed and discerning introductory essay, Muthesius presented a large selection of well-chosen examples, discussed and illustrated with plans, in a catalog accompanying handsome, large photographic plates. In this volume Richard Norman Shaw received particular attention. The second work, *Die neuere kirchliche Baukunst in England* (Recent religious architecture in England), was of equal intelligence but less elaborate; it treated recent English church building, tracing its development from the Gothic revival to Muthesius's own time. Here John Loughborough Pearson was singled out for his revival of true masonry vaulting. The third work, produced after Muthesius's return to Germany and following the publication of *Stilarchitektur*, was the magisterial three-volume study of the English house *Das englische Haus*, which to this day remains without equal. After surveying earlier British domestic architecture, it presented an extensive study of nineteenth-century English residential architecture, notably the "free architecture" of the later part of the century. Every aspect of the English house was considered; the entire third volume emphasized technical issues. In addition to these major works, Muthesius, who wrote indefatigably throughout his life, prepared numerous articles for journals, periodically collecting some of these essays in small volumes.[5]

When he returned to Germany, Muthesius entered the Prussian Ministry of Commerce where he became a prime mover in educational innovation connected with the crafts and architecture and in promoting the relation of artistic culture to industrial society. He was central to the founding of the Deutsche Werkbund in 1907. When released from his duties in the Prussian ministry in 1904, he established his architectural practice, which was most notable for villas, often of considerable proportion and usually situated in the wooded, elegant western fringe of Berlin.[6]

The First World War all but upended the career and program of Muthesius, including his efforts for the Deutsche Werkbund. He continued to write and propagandize about the house and domestic culture but no longer from a leading position. Nevertheless, *Wie baue ich mein Haus?* (How do I build my house?), an elegant handbook of 1917, was his most popular book,[7] and *Kann ich auch jetzt noch mein Haus bauen?* (Can I still build my own house?), 1920, sought to maintain the endeavor in more straitened times and included consideration of row houses and housing estates (*Siedlungen*).[8] Hermann Muthesius died in 1927.

THE NECESSITY OF CULTURAL RENEWAL

A s seen in *STILARCHITEKTUR*, Muthesius was a well-informed admirer of English architecture of the last half of the nineteenth century. Through his work as a cultural attaché of the German Embassy in London and as an architect, he gave careful attention to every aspect of English architectural culture. An avid student of English architecture, he knew its history from the Gothic revival to his own time.

He studied and wrote on all building types, distinctive and new techniques of building construction, new mechanical services, English cities, and the training of architects. His attention to handicrafts was extensive, for he respected and drew inspiration from the careers and work of John Ruskin, William Morris, and the Arts and Crafts Movement in general. Yet in a fundamental way, Muthesius parted company with his English mentors. With the advantage of a temporal and cultural distance and at a moment of renewed attention to the crafts in progressive circles on the Continent, Muthesius saw clearly that Morris's guild activity necessarily led to a condition that defeated his own principles. Morris's work and that of his followers became the possession of a cultural elite and even of the modern industrial culture that the Arts and Crafts Movement had sought to deflect.

Although Muthesius was critical of the nineteenth century, he would not deny its dominant forces: reason, science, technology, industry, and commerce. For him the problem was the one-sided dominance of these forces. Writing at the turn of the century, he observed the popular and academic desire to characterize the previous century. Rejecting global descriptions based on its positive features, he instead settled on "the inartistic century." The dominant forces of science and industry had contributed to this result, but Muthesius's extended account of this lamentable state was internal to the world of art and culture.

Muthesius pointed to the "second artistic revolution" in Western culture (the first having been the Italian Renaissance), which for him was the discovery, or indeed the idealistic fabrication, of Greece. The prime movers of this most recent period of art, which extended through the nineteenth century, were perceived to be Johann Joachim Winckelmann and the classicizing search for stylistic purity: agents undermining artistic creativity by elevating the imitation of ideal models.[9] Even the reactions against Neoclassicism partook of similar faults, for resistance came not in the call for artistic invention but in the claims for a superior precedent—most notably in northern Europe and the Gothic revival. In works of major theoreticians and practitioners of the Gothic revival, Muthesius recognized valid arguments and indeed practices based on principle, that is, arguments that were still instructive. Nonetheless this retrospective position recalls not only the nineteenth century's failure to cope with the new productive forces but also, as already noted with Morris, its devolution into style imitation as an end in itself. From Muthesius's perspective, art and handicrafts lost their footing and survived only in the imitation of an ever broader range of historical forms. A degenerate battle of the styles ensued, leading to an inevitable—yet at that moment only recent—arrival at nothingness.

Muthesius's general orientation, and certainly that of *Stilarchitektur*, was to direct attention to the failure of the arts, and thus to promote heavily the renewal of artistic culture as the vehicle for cultural and social reform more generally. It is such a program that allied Muthesius with Morris and the English Arts and Crafts Movement. The difference for Muthesius, and the German movement of which he was to be a significant figure, was the relationship of art and culture to the system of industrial and technological production. Where the English program broke under its self-imposed demand to resist modern change, Muthesius looked to restore a whole culture through an aspiring artistic production consistent with the emerging industrial society.

Muthesius opened the second and programmatic part of *Stilarchitektur* with a recognition that the conditions and seeds of a new spirit already existed in the recent example of England and now on the Continent, quite particularly in Germany. Architecture should be central to this new development, but because of its ponderous nature it had thus far not been able to take the lead. The new movement in the arts and crafts, with its beginnings in England, had prepared the way not only in the reestablishment of the relation of production to product but also in a social transformation consistent with larger political forces. A "spiritual aristocracy" that stemmed from and represented the new primacy of the middle class now took the lead. The expanded goal of the new movement would be "the creation of a contemporary middle-class art," characterized by sincerity, *Sachlichkeit,*[10] and a purified artistic sensibility. The crafts and the "free architecture" of England (liberated from canons) offered precedents; the challenge was to achieve this art under modern conditions without sliding into "secondary considerations and superficialities," which Muthesius already discerned within the contemporary movements of Art Nouveau. If art was to avoid such superficialities and ever again aspire to the position it had held in the great epochs, then architecture, still properly the mother of the arts, must assume leadership in the community of the arts.

Such programs for cultural renewal were, of course, frequently advanced after Friedrich Nietzsche mounted his brilliant attack on the positivistic science and history that he saw as so dominant within the cultural fabric of nineteenth-century Germany. When Nietzsche envisioned a better German society, he reckoned that the first generation of this new society would have to be brought up with the "mighty truth" that Germany could not build a culture on the basis of this positivistic education. In contrast to mere knowledge about culture (the German's desire "for the flower without the root or the stalk"), art and a genuine culture must spring from a natural ground. "Life itself is a kind of handicraft that must be learned thoroughly and industriously, and diligently practised," Nietzsche wrote. "'Give me life, and I will soon make you a culture out of it'—will be the cry of every man in this new generation, and they will know each other by this cry. But who will give them this life? No god and no man will give it—only their youth."[11]

Nietzsche was the idol of many young artists at the end of the nineteenth century, and even though his words echoed across Europe, his appeal was especially strong in Germany.[12] Just at the time when Nietzsche's writings were becoming common intellectual property, there appeared in 1890 another book that created extraordinary excitement, especially in artistic circles: *Rembrandt als Erzieher* (Rembrandt as educator), written by Julius Langbehn but published anonymously.[13] Langbehn's thought, though certainly influenced by Nietzsche, could hardly compare with the latter's brilliance. Nevertheless, in the decades around 1900 the ideas and influence of these two men commingled. The comparatively shallow and prosaic program of Langbehn, which urged the synthesis of an artistic culture capable of resolving the antinomy of a lost age of faith and a spiritless age of science, could be more easily and purposively grasped than the writings of Nietzsche. Muthesius himself, on the first page of *Kultur und Kunst* (Culture and art), 1904,[14] mentioned the works of both Langbehn and Konrad Lange.[15] He then named the Darmstadt Artists' Colony as a demonstration of the early fruition of these ideas. As late as 1911, Muthesius cited the generative influence of Langbehn's book in an address to the Deutsche Werkbund.

Young enthusiasts for the new artistic movement appropriated these critiques in response to what they felt was a fragmented, incoherent, and artless civilization. Such negative characteristics were seen in the divorce of the artist from society. The dominance of easel painting and of sculpture intended for solitary contemplation in the laboratory atmosphere of museums and salons was interpreted as Western civilization's tendency to render art submissive. Proponents of the new movement felt that the work of art must be removed from its aesthetic, physical, and psychological isolation, even if this endangered the independence of the artist. Creating decorative design that would foster a meaningful environment was considered a higher calling than producing individual works that lacked a social role. The artist might become an architect in order to control his environment; painting and sculpture should be made to play a part in this larger program. The effort to realize such goals brought about an emphasis on the decorative; the very words *decorative* and *ornamental* took on exalted meaning. These artists thus turned away from the culturally divisive fine arts, taking up the decorative arts, which were then acclaimed for contributing to the formation of a superior culture. It was in just such a general cultural ambience that Muthesius, with his exposure to the English movement, began to challenge specifics of the Continental movement—especially the formalist reliance on "decorative" embellishment.

MUTHESIUS'S CRITIQUE OF THE ENGLISH MODEL

ONE MUST LOOK MORE CAREFULLY at Muthesius's asserted English model to understand his advocacy. At this time no one, not even in England, had examined nineteenth-century English crafts and architecture with the depth of Muthesius. The path, however, had been opened by others, as was extensively demonstrated by Stefan Muthesius, Hermann's grandnephew. He used the chapter title "Deutschland unter englischen Einfluss, 1880–1897" (Germany under English influence, 1880–1897) in his book *Das englische Vorbild* (The English Model), thus referring to the period prior to Hermann Muthesius's arrival in London.[16] The most significant publication of this earlier phase was Robert Dohme's *Das englische Haus*, 1888, which exalted as principles the attributes of the emerging suburban and rural English house: the selection of site; orientation of rooms to sun and wind; light and air; cheerfulness; and above all, comfort, convenience, and privacy.[17] Dohme preceded Muthesius in his favorable regard for the Queen Anne style, especially the work of Shaw. Dohme even anticipated the argument of bringing the rational thinking of distinctively modern production to the house, as when he claimed that the English in their architecture emulated what was achieved internationally in the efficient outfitting of ships and railroad cars.[18]

As Muthesius pushed forward in his documentation of the English dwelling, however, he was compelled by events to develop his related advocacy for Germany. He then found it necessary to criticize the English model and offer alternatives. Nonetheless, the underlying appreciation of the English accomplishment was not lost because Muthesius found at the root of the English movement a social and indeed an ethnic position that he deemed to be common to the peoples of northern Europe. The successful efforts of Inigo Jones and a century later the Palladians to impose on the English a foreign, Mediterranean, and classical architecture of purist standards provided a natural immunity to a powerful Neoclassicism such as that which had dominated Germany in the first half of the nineteenth century.[19] Furthermore, England had never fully lost its competence with the Gothic—notwithstanding the prominence of Palladianism in high architecture and as both an urban and rural vernacular. Then, too, the Romantic Movement in literature and art blossomed early and in a manner unique to England. Consequently the "Romantic building-art," which Muthesius equated with the appreciation of the Gothic, was early, strong, and dominant over the classic in England.[20]

Significantly allied to religious reform and renewal, church building in England thrived under bourgeois patronage, supporting the development of a major Gothic revival. With Pearson, who was particularly important for the revival of masonry vaulting, Muthesius saw the achievement of a "genuinely Nordic building-art."[21] Muthesius nonetheless faulted the English Gothicists' search for Gothic handicrafts and their attempts to adapt Gothic architecture to secular buildings. Quite simply, he noted, "no new Gothic tradition would develop."[22]

Through yet another twist, Muthesius argued that the English did indeed create "a modern and national art." With this claim, we return to Ruskin and Morris, who built a genuine popular enthusiasm for art with ideals derived from the Gothic. This was accomplished, above all else, by shifting attention away from high art and representation and toward the domestic interior—a humble genre that promoted the ideals of sound workmanship, reasonableness, and sincerity. The primacy of the domestic interior to the entire reformulation of modern culture and art, as established by Morris, reached a freer and fuller level in the houses of Shaw and the Queen Anne revival. It is here that Muthesius found the beginning of the new architectural movement. To observe this larger vision, we can do no better than to recite Muthesius's enthusiastic and programmatic assessment of the Queen Anne.

> It was nothing other than a rejection of architectural formalism in favor of a simple and natural, reasonable way of building. One brought nothing new to such a movement; everything had existed for centuries in the vernacular architecture of the small town and rural landscape . . . one found all that one desired and for which one thirsted: adaptation to needs and local conditions, unpretentiousness and honesty of feeling; utmost coziness and comfort in the layout of rooms, color, an uncommonly attractive and painterly (but also reasonable) design, and an economy in building construction. The new English domestic building-art that developed on this basis has now produced valuable results. But it has also done more: it has spread the interest and the understanding for domestic architecture to the entire people. It has created the only sure foundation for a new artistic culture: the artistic house. And as everyone connected with the Arts and Crafts Movement in England certainly knows, it produced that for which everyone labored: the English house.[23]

Thus in this innovative establishment of a high architecture based upon the house, Muthesius found the key to artistic and cultural renewal allied both to his convictions of social change under modern industrial society and to his desire for an appropriately distinctive culture of the northern, particularly the Germanic, peoples.

With this northern European emphasis on the domestic interior of the middle-class home, we may recognize an ambiguity in the historical saga of the first part of *Stilarchitektur*. In England, as in the German-speaking lands, the late eighteenth century and the time around 1800 constituted an important period for the development of middle-class, and even lower middle-class, society. For this time and this social class, the locus of art and culture was the house and the domestic interior—in the more vernacular versions of Neoclassicism and in what is known as Biedermeier. Notwithstanding his efforts to distinguish a proper northern culture from that of the Mediterranean, Muthesius appreciated this classicizing domestic culture of the esteemed epoch of Goethe. For Muthesius, an important aspect of this culture in England had been the development of a distinctive, indigenous, middle-class furniture: Chippendale, Hepplewhite, and Sheraton. In England, as in Germany, this eighteenth-century, middle-class art had collapsed by 1850. Muthesius saw this rupture as significantly related to the advent of the machine and the decline of handicrafts, particularly in furniture production but also in architecture.

Yet it is also at this point that Muthesius sought to pick up a thread of development different from that of his admired English predecessors. Despite the debasement of taste engendered by the surfeit of machine-made surrogate objects, and despite the consequent suppression of the crafts and of artisanal authenticity, the machine was not the necessary evil that the English movement claimed. In the appropriation of the machine, as in the economical advantages offered by transportation, constructional technologies, new materials such as iron and glass, and new building types, Muthesius found the components for an emerging new architecture. The English failure to embrace these new realities had not only limited its reformational development but also defeated its social agenda. Inevitably, the Arts and Crafts Movement became an artistic production for the elite; middle-class interests were not served. In contrast, Muthesius envisioned higher standards of quality through industrial production and predicted the desired reestablishment of the integrity and pride of the worker.

ART NOUVEAU AND JUGENDSTIL

Brussels in the 1890s energetically embraced and assimilated new artistic forces, whether from Postimpressionist painting in France or from arts-and-crafts production in England. Distinctive new directions emerged in Belgium with the architecture of Victor Horta and with the designs and architectural essays of Henry van de Velde. By the late 1890s van de Velde had also established a strong base in Germany, both associating with and competing against new tendencies there. In

Munich, Vienna, and Berlin, the Secessionist Movements supported new art, increasingly identified with crafts and architecture. Glossy new magazines that were particularly devoted to the "decorative arts" appeared in these cities and in Darmstadt where, by the turn of the century, the prince became a major patron of the new movement through his creation of the artists' colony and its distinctive environment, which was conceived as *Ein Dokument Deutscher Kunst* (A document of German art).

Even this abbreviated list of the events in Germany circa 1900 indicates that Muthesius's advocacy of reform fell on well-prepared soil. But this was also a problem. By 1902 these new movements (known in Germany, somewhat ambivalently, as Jugendstil, or "youth style") were being rapidly depreciated, and not solely by the philistines. The Darmstadt Artists' Colony was severely criticized; rather than becoming a formative event, it established at best a plateau deserted by one of its luminaries, Peter Behrens. The International Exposition of Decorative Arts held in Turin in 1902 suffered an even harsher critical assessment. In this critical climate, Van de Velde's position was put on the defensive and never again achieved its earlier degree of conviction or influence.

Since the doubts about the Jugendstil and Art Nouveau movements centered on premature and excessively individualistic attempts at new artistic form-making, or even at defining a style, Muthesius's preferred precedents and his position could be taken as a tonic. Yet if his envisioned movement were to succeed, he needed the energy of these forces for renewal and, conversely, could not afford to be associated solely with a conservative resistance to the new.

The negative pole of the title of Muthesius's book, *Stilarchitektur*, asserted again a resistance to the "battle of the styles" of the nineteenth century, a battle that had resulted in the devaluation of all earlier modes of building and finally left the architect with "nothingness." If nothingness was to be avoided, this stylistic pursuit could only seek to offer a "new style." There had been a famous and often-derided attempt at a new style in the competition for the Maximilianstrasse in Munich in 1851,[24] and there were related discussions in the later decades of the nineteenth century. Now it was possible, and in this Muthesius joined, to see the Jugendstil as just what its name seemed to indicate: the proffering of a new and already failing style. For many of its practitioners the danger for the new movement in the arts and crafts was, in fact, the search for new forms, and thus for a new style, before a fundamental reassessment of the condition of contemporary artistic production had been achieved or even attempted.

So the Jugendstil and, quite explicitly, the thought and work of van de Velde, came under the criticism of Muthesius, who interpreted it as the last and least supportable version of "style-architecture." Worst of all was the contemporary phenomenon whereby lesser artists and manufacturers took to imitating such new, individual styles. The historical styles at least possessed a currency based on known and shared conventions; nothing could contribute less to art or to society, Muthesius reasoned, than casting into the popular market exemplars of "art for art's sake." Upon reflection, he noted with satisfaction that the nineteenth century as the century of styles had altogether devalued the style instinct.[25]

So Muthesius asserted that the genuine values of the crafts and the building-art were wholly independent of style and of this forced form-making; for him it was just as well that the whiplash line—Muthesius's shorthand for Jugendstil formalism—had been so quickly debased.[26] He doubted that such formal systems were intrinsically allied to any modern sensibility, and if they were, he questioned who would tie new forms of production to the fleeting moments of this shifting ground. What might be appropriate as accomplished poetry, music, or even unique ornament could not serve the prosaic needs of the everyday to which the crafts and the building-art must be directed. Muthesius argued for a production appropriate for the majority of the population, one endowed with the attributes of the matter-of-fact (sachlich), rational, and realistic. At the point of acknowledging that crafts were still a matter of form, he also pointed out that unornamented form was not necessarily inartistic. "What we need is not an emotion-laden furniture and a luxurious art but decent household artifacts for the ordinary man."[27] As he argued more generally: "The well-being and the hope of the future lies in this: in the conceptual bonding of arts and crafts to subdue 'art' in the recovery of a suitable craft production."[28]

If Muthesius had clearly sought to distinguish his advocacy from the formal excesses of Jugendstil, he required other distinctions within his own models and program: those of production and of social construction. The debasement of Jugendstil may have been hastened in its adoption by industry, but in its origins it was not closely tied to any argument for or against industrial production. Muthesius's English references required a reformulation to elude the anti-industrial thrust of that movement. He found an argument that addressed both these issues: "The machine does not exist in order to produce art. This is a privilege of the human hand . . . the human hand can use tools. . . . The machine is, however, only an improved tool."[29]

Allied with this shift in attitude toward industrial production is the ambiguity of Muthesius's social advocacy. Despite references to improving the ethos of industrial work or addressing the environmental needs of the greater number, Muthesius's viewpoint was far from Morris's socialism. Muthesius was also aware of, and indeed took no pleasure in, the irony of English arts-and-crafts production becoming the property of an elite, which offered little, even indirectly, to the working class or lower middle class.

In contrast, it is through his attention to the environmental needs of the larger population in everyday life and the allied exploitation of modern means of production that Muthesius sought a more effective social program than that which the Arts and Crafts Movement had achieved. Even if it is a reflection of his realpolitik, one must note that Muthesius framed this issue explicitly in terms of the middle class.

Despite these distinctions, England remained a positive model for Muthesius for two major reasons. First, if he argued that unornamented form could still be artistic, exemplars continued to be helpful in resisting the formalism of the Jugendstil. In England's free architecture, from Morris and Philip Webb, down to the high achievements of Shaw and the young practitioners of his own day, Muthesius perceived a formal restraint that fortified his resolve and provided models. Second, the centrality of domestic architecture to the English movement offered evidence that the new movement (in England as well as on the Continent) could affect social and cultural conditions quite generally, not only for an elite and not only in matters of high art. Muthesius spoke to both these issues.

> [Germany can do what] was done in England: to return our vernacular building-art to simplicity and naturalness, as is preserved in our old rural buildings; to renounce every architectural trinket on and in our house; and to introduce a sense of spatial warmth, color, natural layout, and sensible configuration instead of continuing to be restrained by the chains of formalistic and academic architecture-mongering. The way in which the English achieved this goal, namely, by readapting vernacular and rural building motifs, promises us the richest harvest—precisely in Germany where the rural building manner of the past is clothed in a poetry and a wealth of sentiment that few old English buildings can match. If we restrict ourselves to the homegrown, and if each of us impartially follows his own individual artistic inclinations, then we will soon have not only a reasonable but also a national, vernacular building-art. Nationality in art need not be artificially bred. If one raises genuine people, we will have a genuine art that for every individual with a sincere character can be nothing other than national. For every genuine person is a part of a genuine nationality.[30]

Although the title and content of *Stilarchitektur* emphasize art and architecture, it is apparent that Muthesius's position takes root in his assessment that German life and culture—the everyday culture of all citizens—had been displaced and debased during the nineteenth century. A new architecture would help to heal these wounds. The role and the character of that architecture was established by this more fundamental cultural concern.

In earlier periods, that is, before the nineteenth century reduced architecture to "styles," Muthesius observed that it was evident how one would live and build through the social and artistic conventions that were so widely shared in those societies. If the nineteenth century was the "inartistic century," Muthesius claimed that no factor was so decisive in judging a time to have been artistic "as the degree to which art is the property of the entire people—to what extent it is an essential part of the cultural endowment of the time."[31] On the evidence of ethnological museums Muthesius found that aboriginal tribes must be termed artistic. From this he argued "that the artistic instinct belongs to the elementary powers of mankind and casts a still more peculiar light on a time such as ours, which has left these powers to wither."[32]

Muthesius saw his society as dominated by parvenu pretension, spending its life in a sham culture, and called for it to divest itself of ostentation. "A genuine art can only rest on genuine feelings. Art is not solely a matter of ability and the exercise of aesthetic feelings but, above all else, a matter of character and sensibility. They must be maintained especially in architecture, the art of daily life."[33]

The endorsement of industrial production was, therefore, more than just a realistic assessment of the conditions of the times. If there were to be an improvement in artistic culture and environment that reached everyone and the everyday, then both the ethos of industrial production and its products had to be engaged. In Muthesius's analysis, using the machine to produce surrogate and shabby objects that compete only by quantity and price forced workers to earn less while demoralizing them in their work. The machine had been misused; it was neither omnipotent nor driven by its own inexorable forces. It was a tool and its products would satisfy when they departed from imitation and became typical machine forms; this had happened with the bicycle, machine tools, iron bridges. The working class, rather than being the producers and consumers of sham objects, must be affected by, indeed enlisted in, the drive for quality in the design and production of objects and the environment in general.

In railroad stations, steamships, and bicycles were to be found the modern ideas and new principles of design that indicated our aesthetic progress: a rigorous, even scientific objectivity (*Sachlichkeit*) with its product, the undecorated *Sachform*. Process and product alike were marked by rationality and the direct satisfaction of need. That this could be observed in modern clothing, and in the generalization of clothing across class, was evidence that a more functional approach to design was characteristic of the time and offered the potential for a shared, authentic culture.

Yet Muthesius was not arguing for a naive functionalism; the satisfaction of purpose alone was insufficient. In both modern clothing and machines he observed a coincidence of aesthetic and sanitary concerns. There was also a retention of details explained not by necessity but by their symbolization of all that "is neat and in the best of order," that is, "a handsome elegance and a certain clean conciseness of form."[34] Indeed Muthesius found this attitude to be universal in modern design; in architecture it was revealed especially in the English house.

MUTHESIUS'S PROGRAM OF *SACHLICHE KUNST*

THE TRANSITION FROM IRON-AND-GLASS railroad terminals to the English house requires an explanation, which may be found in Muthesius's own words. Expounding on his belief that historicist architecture occupied a retrogressive position, he observed:

> While Mother Architecture found herself on a wrong path, life never rested but went on to create forms for the innovations it had produced, the simple forms of pure practicality [*Sachlichkeit*]. It created our machines, vehicles, implements, iron bridges, and glass halls. It led the way soberly in that it proceeded practically—one would like to say purely scientifically. It not only embodied the spirit of the time but also fitted itself to the aesthetic-tectonic views that were reformed under the same influence. These views, ever more decisively than the earlier decorative art, demanded a corresponding, straightforward [*sachlich*] art.[35]

Muthesius thus makes a distinction and a connection between his admiration for the characteristic works of industrial culture and his own position. The former are marked by a pure *Sachlichkeit,* which stems from a nearly scientific design process. This process and these works establish norms for our aesthetic-tectonic views, but he does not expect or advocate an unmodulated transposition of either the process or the forms to other realms of life and design. For him the domestic interior is more fundamental than the railroad shed. Within his vision of an artistic culture, these dissimilar environments must have a correspondence but not an identity. English "free architecture" offered the best exemplars of domestic interiors possessing such a correspondence. The year before the publication of *Stilarchitektur*, Muthesius had already joined the noted critic Julius Meier-Graefe in praising a new suite of interiors by Rudolph Alexander Schröder in Munich (fig. 2) that not only provided

2. RUDOLF ALEXANDER SCHRÖDER WITH MARTIN DÜLFER AND
PAUL LUDWIG TROOST, VESTIBULE, HEYMEL APARTMENT, MU-
NICH, 1899–1901. FROM *DEKORATIVE KUNST* 4, NO. 7 (APRIL
1901): 249. SANTA MONICA, THE GETTY CENTER FOR THE HIS-
TORY OF ART AND THE HUMANITIES.

a concrete example on German soil but might even be seen to have advanced the cause.[36] In Muthesius's assessment, these interiors "appear to realize all the ideals of a genuine new art and in their simple comfort and unornamented amplitude represent a true reinvigoration."[37]

Harry Mallgrave has pointed to a text by Richard Streiter of 1896 that reads as a theoretical basis for Meier-Graefe and Muthesius:

> *Realism* in architecture is the comprehensive consideration of the real constituents of a building, the most complete fulfillment of the demands of functionality, comfort, and health—in one word: practicality [*Sachlichkeit*]. But this is not all. Just as realism in poetry views as one of its central tasks the delineation of character in relation to its milieu, so the parallel program in architecture sees as its most desirable goal of artistic truth the development of the character of a building not only out of the determination of its needs but also from the milieu—from the qualities of local materials and from the environmentally and historically conditioned atmosphere of the place [*Stimmung der Oertlichkeit*].[38]

In advocating simplicity and a straightforward approach to design, especially in comparison with the excesses of late historicism or the ornamental tendencies of the Jugendstil, Muthesius, as Streiter before him, employed such concepts to signify the generation of form from need, health considerations, materials, and construction. Proponents of this position also advocated artlessness and elimination of ornament. Even though they could often appreciate engineering works of a pure objectivity (*Sachlichkeit*), as was the case with Muthesius, they asked for something more: something real not haunted by the apparition of the ideal but rather the interplay of invention, or convention, with the material world, facilitating a creatively evolving cultural setting. It is this which Streiter called character and milieu, Meier-Graefe atmosphere and milieu; and it is this which Muthesius found in English interiors.[39]

It is precisely because the program of Muthesius had its roots in this search for conventions shared by the entire society, and thus was at base a social advocacy, that he placed the domestic interior and the house above all else in the definition of a new movement in architecture. Muthesius sought to establish this type of domestic culture, already well advanced in England, in its own indigenous form in Germany. Yet he wavered between the possibilities and difficulties of this enterprise. To the extent that this cultural work might depend on models in the vernacular of the preindustrial town and the countryside, we have already seen that he considered Germany to have a number of more profound models. In Germany on the other hand, there was not a culture of the house to compare with that of England. He lamented that Germans of his time characteristically lived in rental apartments, often moving from one to another, and thus experienced little or no connection with their surroundings or concern that these be artistically designed. Nonetheless, he concluded that "a change in our German artistic situation can only take its start in the German house, which essentially is yet to be created."[40] He preferred to move from the small to the large. People could design their individual rooms in a reasonable and artistic (second edition: "tasteful") manner. From this nascent sensibility Muthesius felt that a more genuine and popular feeling for the house could be awakened in the German people. It is first by successfully addressing this problem that society could bring this sensitivity for art[41] to the street and larger environment and ultimately to the public at large, not only in the multiplicity of its individual dwellings but also in its public realms. He argued that architecture must serve social life, everyday problems.

Patronage, as much in the new movement (Jugendstil) as in the historicism against which it fought, was dominantly motivated by a desire for pomp, display, and admiration. On the contrary, "The new art cannot be engaged with such patronage. If it wants to better the world, it must turn to broader circles."[42]

While Muthesius's advocacy was not alienated from industrial production, it was also not complacent or uncritical. He insisted that the public must comprehend quality and require it in resisting the tendencies of factory owners. Progress in the arts and in a reinvigorated culture necessitated that people again acquire an understanding of quality, a yet uninaugurated matter of fundamental public education. Quality resided in what was essential: "authenticity of form in the conception, material, and production of the arts and crafts," a condition necessary before one could even speak of raising the object into the realm of art.[43]

Muthesius sought this same authenticity for architecture, both for its own integrity and because it could win the public approbation necessary for cultural advance. First in the epigraph from Morris and then recurrently in *Stilarchitektur*, the proper models for a new and genuine architecture could only be "necessary, unpretentious buildings." Such were the simple, matter-of-fact (*sachlich*) burghers' houses of the time around 1800, "which still could serve as a model for our contemporary conditions."[44] Such also was the vernacular building-art of preindustrial times when there was a proper distinction between the non-monumental and the monumental. Such were also the structures of nineteenth-century commerce and transport.

It was Muthesius's view that in such works were to be found the signs of an aesthetic progress that can only be achieved by paying strict attention to matters of fact (the *Sachlichen*). Yet contemporary architecture for the most part refused that which was valid elsewhere, thus alienating itself from life. This is what he meant by the terms *architecture-mongering* and *style-mongering*. The painterliness of the German Renaissance revival was as much in error as the artificial symmetry of the Italian style. A master builder should attend only to what a particular type of building required:

> When he seeks only to do justice, and indeed in every detail, to those demands presented by the site, the construction, the design of the rooms, by the ordering of the windows, doors, heating and lighting sources—then we would already be on the way to that strict straight-forwardness [*strengen Sachlichkeit*] that we have come to recognize as the basic feature of modern sensibility.[45]

According to Muthesius, the new movement took account of every circumstance, fluently adapting to every need, to the inner essence of the problem, and it sought to express these demands outwardly. Instead of a pedantic, academic, and generalizing approach, the new movement individualized the process. For Muthesius, such individualization was characteristic of the contemporary spirit that the movement embraced. Rather than style, the new movement should treat materials according to their nature and with sound workmanship and continue its pursuit of a unity of form and color. Muthesius's opposition to style thus had at least three sources: a concept of expression that he associated with the new movement, the exemplars of objectivity (pure *Sachlichkeit*), and his most synthetic constructions of realist art (*sachliche Kunst*).

Muthesius saw one positive influence extending from the rehearsal of styles in the nineteenth century to the new movement. The very eclecticism of that time introduced an appreciation of matching formal attributes with the use of a space or a building. If under the sway of the styles this matching was done primarily through association, the new movement could nonetheless draw on this positive, individualizing drive and freely seek a reasonable relation of building type or function of individual spaces to innovative systems of form and color.

Recurrently in *Stilarchitektur* the only source for a generalizing characterization of the visual culture of modern times is found not in any style but rather in the objects, machines, and constructions in the service of new systems. But even these works cannot be distilled into a style of the time, for the lesson they teach is that of process, and once this process was itself adapted and employed for different social purposes—the dwelling, for example—it would yield different forms.

It is this last step—the move to a *sachliche Kunst*, or a realist architecture—that most engaged Muthesius. Here, not only the particularities of the site, material, climate, and occupant but also the differentiations of region and nation preclude the definition of a style.

Thus while Muthesius recognized a "pure" *Sachlichkeit* in the machines and iron constructions of the nineteenth century, he was not advocating this pure *Sachlichkeit* but the *sachliche Kunst* that he respected in English domestic architecture. Muthesius was, therefore, consistent with Streiter's realism and with Meier-Graefe's and his own endorsement of Schröder's interiors when he commended "the now-apparent need to acknowledge the special attributes of a building, to characterize the particular kind of space *architecturally*."[46]

COMPARISON OF THE TWO EDITIONS

THE PRECEDING EXPOSITION of *Stilarchitektur und Baukunst* has treated the text as if it existed in a single edition and has made only occasional reference to the second edition of 1903. This seems justified on two grounds: the quick succession of the two editions and, more importantly, the maintenance of the principal argument in the two editions.

In the foreword to the second edition Muthesius stated that *Stilarchitektur* conveyed the content of two lectures delivered in the winter of 1901. Indeed, although the title page of the first edition is dated 1902, the cover of that edition bears the date 1901. The foreword of the second edition was dated August 1903.

Notwithstanding the brief interval between the editions, these years represent a period of dynamic change for matters of concern to Muthesius. In 1901 the Vienna Secession was at the peak of its activity; during this time even the work of the Viennese master Wagner was marked by the decorative approach of that movement. Also in 1901 the living and working environment of the Darmstadt Artists' Colony, built to the designs of the Viennese architect Joseph Olbrich but also incorporating the house and theatrical program of Behrens, opened and commanded attention. Its ambition was to influence the future artistic environment of Germany quite generally. The theoretical and formal programs of van de Velde seemed still in ascendancy. Art Nouveau was a significant aspect of the International Exposition held in Paris in 1901. The success of these programs was, of course, also the occasion for reassessment and criticism, including strong criticism among the leading figures who regretted the effects of the popular success of this work among lesser artists and producers. Muthesius's lectures of winter 1901, which formed the basis of

3. COVER FROM THE FIRST EDITION OF HERMANN MUTHE-
SIUS'S *STILARCHITEKTUR UND BAUKUNST* (1902; THE COVER IN-
CORRECTLY BEARS THE DATE 1901). SANTA MONICA, THE GETTY
CENTER FOR THE HISTORY OF ART AND THE HUMANITIES.

HERMANN MUTHESIUS

STILARCHITEKTUR UND BAUKUNST

WANDLUNGEN
DER ARCHITEKTUR IM XIX.
JAHRHUNDERT UND IHR
HEUTIGER STANDPUNKT

MÜLHEIM-RUHR 1902
VERLAG VON K. SCHIMMELPFENG

4. TITLE PAGE FROM THE FIRST EDITION OF HERMANN MUTHE-
SIUS'S *STILARCHITEKTUR UND BAUKUNST* (1902). SANTA MON-
ICA, THE GETTY CENTER FOR THE HISTORY OF ART AND THE
HUMANITIES.

ich glaube, dass das Gedeihen unserer Maler- und Bild-
hauerschulen in erster Linie von dem Gedeihen unserer
Architektur abhängig ist. Alle Künste müssen solange im
Schwächezustande verharren, bis diese bereit sein wird,
die Führung wieder zu übernehmen."

Wann wird unsere Architektur hierzu bereit sein?
Nicht eher jedenfalls, als bis sie sich aus den Fesseln
des Stilgesichtspunktes, in denen sie während eines Jahrhunderts festgebannt lag, zu neuer goldener Freiheit empor-
gerungen hat, nicht eher, als bis sie aus einer schemen-
haften Stilarchitektur wieder zu einer lebendigen Baukunst
geworden ist.

67

5. DECORATIVE DEVICE FROM THE FIRST EDITION OF HER-
MANN MUTHESIUS'S *STILARCHITEKTUR UND BAUKUNST* (1902).
SANTA MONICA, THE GETTY CENTER FOR THE HISTORY OF ART
AND THE HUMANITIES.

Stilarchitektur, count among such early criticisms both in their general mistrust of the formalism and decorative excess of this new movement and in their specific criticism of van de Velde. Still, the most likely agents of Muthesius's own position would emerge from among these same practitioners, and if there were to be cultural change in wider circles, Muthesius could not encourage a general mistrust of innovation. Thus his criticisms of Jugendstil were directed to perceived excesses while at the same time he extolled the potential of the new movement.

This is an appropriate place to note changes in the graphic style of the two editions of *Stilarchitectur und Baukunst*. The first edition surprisingly bears Jugendstil ornaments on the cover, title page, and beginnings and endings of the text sections (figs. 3–5). The colors of the cloth cover, blue ornaments and gold lettering on green fabric, are also characteristic of Art Nouveau. Since the most elaborate of these ornaments, that seen on the cover, features the initials of the publisher, I suggest that the graphics are owing to the publisher rather than revealing an inconsistency between Muthesius's thought and presentation. In any case, the second edition of only about one year later,[47] is printed without ornaments; the cover is of blue boards (figs. 6, 7). Admittedly this was an inexpensive edition, but the changes are surely owing to Muthesius's position and the rapidly declining fortunes of the Jugendstil.

By 1902 conditions had changed. The Viennese architects restrained their more decorative instincts and began to take a more abstract and tectonic approach. The bloom of the Darmstadt Artists' Colony very quickly wilted; criticism intensified as Behrens accepted a teaching post in the arts and crafts at the Kunstgewerbeschule in Düsseldorf. Van de Velde was also retrenching and found little success in his scientized exhibition called *Linie und Form* (Line and form) held at the Kaiser-Wilhelm-Museum in Krefeld in 1904. The International Exposition of Decorative Arts held in Turin in 1902 was conceived in the manner of Art Nouveau and suffered in critical acclaim precisely because of that fact.

Consequently, when Muthesius reworked *Stilarchitektur* in 1903, his *sachlich* alternative to Art Nouveau was more compelling and was aided by the forceful decline of enthusiasm for Jugendstil. He took complete advantage of the situation, as we see in the foreword to the second edition. Acknowledging that the new movement began in the applied arts, he noted the continuing success of journalism in "the field of the wrongly termed 'decorative art.'" Without rejecting such journalism, which could be of the greatest assistance, he sought to move it away from the "decorative," and even to move beyond something that had appeared significantly in the first edition of *Stilarchitektur*, the "artistic interior." He now insisted that "the central issue of the new artistic movement is architecture."[48]

These terminological changes and the shift away from Jugendstil and even

6. COVER FROM THE SECOND EDITION OF HERMANN MUTHE-
SIUS'S *STILARCHITEKTUR UND BAUKUNST* (1903). BIBLIOTHEK
WERNER OECHSLIN.

HERMANN MUTHESIUS

STILARCHITEKTUR
UND BAUKUNST

WANDLUNGEN DER ARCHITEKTUR
UND DER GEWERBLICHEN KÜNSTE
IM NEUNZEHNTEN JAHRHUNDERT
UND IHR HEUTIGER STANDPUNKT

ZWEITE STARK VERMEHRTE AUFLAGE

MÜLHEIM AN DER RUHR 1903
VERLAG VON K. SCHIMMELPFENG

7. TITLE PAGE FROM THE SECOND EDITION OF HERMANN MU-
THESIUS'S *STILARCHITEKTUR UND BAUKUNST* (1903). BIBLIO-
THEK WERNER OECHSLIN.

from the arts and crafts are notable in the revised text. Already in the second paragraph what had been a positive reference to "the controlling decorative rule" that ordered the arts under architecture becomes simply "the controlling rule." More startling are other changes in that same paragraph: "The minor arts, even with the happy impulse they received [second edition: 'in Germany'] at the end of the nineteenth century, spin helplessly this way and that, and will do so as long as the refuge of the great Mother Architecture—in this case the artistic [second edition: 'German'] dwelling—is lacking."[49] These two references to Germany are new: the first is the notably chauvinistic claim for the "happy" development of the minor arts; the second is the redirection of Muthesius's cause from the "artistic dwelling" (admittedly to be reconceived within German culture) to the emphatically "German dwelling." Toward the end of *Stilarchitektur*, where Muthesius previously had lauded the English for the centrality to their movement of "the artistic house," he now recognized "the national house." This is followed by a sentence in the first edition that reads: "In contrast, our new Continental movement will have to wander in journals and exhibitions until we Germans will finally have an artistic house." This becomes simply "a house," effectively replacing "artistic" with an implicit "German."[50]

The only major addition to Part 1 of *Stilarchitektur* is a new paragraph that brings Muthesius's historical account more into line with this increased mistrust of artistic formalism and the appreciation of a simple and German architecture. In both editions the Rococo of the eighteenth century is admired for providing a system of forms such that all arts and crafts and all social classes shared in a common sensibility. In the second edition a new sentence emphatically assures us that the classical (thus Mediterranean) roots of the Rococo had been fully assimilated to the place and time of German Rococo. More important is the addition of a new paragraph under the heading "Middle-Class Art." This is an appreciation of the vernacular classicism of the period following the Rococo, acclaimed as "simple, *sachlich*, and reasonable," an architecture as common and widespread as the burghers of Germany and "which still could serve as a model for our contemporary conditions."[51]

The only extensive textual change in Part 2 of *Stilarchitektur* is the reworking of three paragraphs from the first edition into thirty paragraphs in the second edition. In the foreword to the latter edition Muthesius, despite his increased insistence on architecture, characterized this addition as "a supplement on the condition of the arts and crafts." Here he is at pains to distinguish what is good in the new movement and "the new interior," for example, color; a greater abstraction; and simplicity as opposed to the whiplash (or Belgian) line, the ornament craze, and the pretensions of Jugendstil. In the latter he recognizes a sham culture that is then extended to the masses through machine-made surrogates. Such production, shoddy in its conception and fabrication, depreciates not only the artistic movement but also the ethos of the working class and living conditions of the citizenry in general.[52]

This misuse of machine fabrication leads Muthesius into his analysis of the machine as a tool that, when controlled by the pursuit of quality in design and production, can be a positive force for the cultural transformation he seeks. He nevertheless returns to an analysis of a present German culture that is more marked by its difficulties than by its positive qualities: the disjuncture between art and life even among the advocates of the new movement, the search for pomp and display, an art of emotion ridiculed in its reduction to "emotion-laden furniture," and a fundamental absence of a German understanding of the house, which is only partially explained by the prevalence of the rental apartment. The obverse of these complaints is his insistence that a *sachlich* sensibility must be the possession of the middle class and inform the desired transformation of German culture.[53] A notable summary of that position follows:

> If [the new art] wants to better the world, it must turn to broader circles. Its particular goal can only be our middle class. The wind that today blows across our culture is middle class. Just as today we all work, just as everyone's clothing is middle class, just as our new tectonic forms (insofar as they are not the work of architects) move in the track of complete simplicity and straightforwardness [*Sachlichkeit*], so also we want to live in middle-class rooms whose essence and goal is simplicity and straightforwardness. No limits are set to good taste within these forms of straightforwardness; indeed here it can be engaged more genuinely than in the worn out, ostentatious cramming of our houses today.[54]

STILARCHITEKTUR IN THE LITERATURE OF THE TIME

I N A CONTEMPORARY REVIEW of *Stilarchitektur und Baukunst*, the Viennese critic Joseph August Lux found this small tract to speak volumes in defining the decisive turning point at which the new movement in art and architecture had arrived.[55] Muthesius's book was an engaged and economical draft of a history and a preferred tendency for a later movement that proved to be significant especially in its attention to the machine and industry. Nevertheless, it was more the economy of the text and its timing than its originality that gave the work its currency.

There is no point in attempting to trace the genealogy of specific arguments in Muthesius, but it is possible to present aspects of the context from which they developed. First, of course, is the English contribution. *Stilarchitektur* begins with an epigraph from Morris, and the text makes ample and positive reference to Augustus Welby Pugin and to Ruskin in particular. These were the key and already well-recognized figures behind the development of late nineteenth-century English thought on artistic culture and architecture. Muthesius rarely mentions figures close to his own generation, so it is perhaps not surprising that we find no reference to William Lethaby, although it is in his thought that this English tradition was freed of much of its decorative excess and oriented toward simpler design and a more accepting attitude toward industrial society. Lethaby was specific in his distaste for "style" and "art," and looked for a straightforward address of life and work. Lethaby's position would be as close to an adequate precedent for that of *Stilarchitektur* as we shall find, but one must still recognize that Muthesius was the leader in giving exposition to English architectural thought and work at the turn of the century.[56] Lethaby himself acknowledged this in a famous lecture given at the Architectural Association in London during World War I, while also acknowledging that England could learn from contemporary German architecture.[57]

Of Muthesius's rare, specific comments on contemporary positions in architecture, the most notable and positive was his commendation of Wagner. "Only in Vienna, where the architecture school of Otto Wagner has already for some years worked toward an architecture that is both artistically freer and more considerate of the demands of purpose, was the building-art both able and inclined from the beginning to form an alliance with the newly arising crafts."[58] There was, however, another tradition in German architectural thought still closer to the position advocated in *Stilarchitektur*. We have already noted this in Muthesius's high regard for the Munich interiors by Schröder, as he came to know them through their publication by Meier-Graefe. Meier-Graefe, wishing to promote related work in an unornamented style, commented: "The movement apparently and hopefully will follow Schröder's path. . . . The Viennese already begin; notably Loos makes furniture without ornament in Vienna and is not without influence."[59] This invites the question of whether Muthesius was or was not one of those with "deaf ears" with regard to the polemical journalism of Adolf Loos in Vienna at the end of the nineteenth century. Although Loos's writings were disseminated more widely only with their publication in book form as *Ins Leere gesprochen* (Spoken into the void), 1921, there was clearly a continuing currency of Loos's thought, which already included many themes found in *Stilarchitektur*: for example, depreciation of the imitative use of styles, early and radical dismissal of the search for a new style in the Secession and Jugendstil, and even such comparative references as their shared attention to modern clothing.[60] But aside from the witty, acerbic, and even pessimistic framing of

Loos's argument, there are also differences in position.[61] Rather than look for Muthesius's direct borrowings from Loos, it is more appropriate to see in this potential relationship one aspect of a concomitant German theoretical and—to a lesser extent—practical tradition favoring a realist architecture. Streiter was also an important theoretician for this position, a fact that has recently received elucidation.[62]

MUTHESIUS AND THE DEUTSCHE WERKBUND

IN MUNICH IN OCTOBER 1907 a group of artists (mainly architects) and producers (at the scale of craft production but soon to be joined by fully industrialized firms) founded the Deutsche Werkbund. This movement was to have wide effect in Germany for the next decade and continues even now.[63] It embodied principles learned from Morris, including the importance of the satisfaction, if not the joy, of workers in their production and the coherent relation of process and product. For the people of the Werkbund, however, it was both possible and necessary to extend Morris's principles to processes entailing a division of labor: the work of the artist-designer, the craftsman-producer, and even the industrial producer.

The Werkbund brought these motifs together under the concept of *Qualität*. Its members believed that by raising the standards of design, using the finest quality materials and the best manual talent (thus creating meaningful work), they would promote a reintegrated cultural environment, which, through the excellence of its products, would allow Germany to compete internationally on the basis of quality rather than quantity.

Such a program will sound familiar to readers of *Stilarchitektur*, and not surprisingly, for Muthesius was among the most active of the founders of the Werkbund. He continued to play a strong role down to his involvement in the famous Werkbund debate just before the outbreak of the First World War. This is not the place to examine the Werkbund in detail, although it deserves notice for it is obvious that much of the Werkbund's important cultural emphasis was already present in the turn-of-the-century thought of Muthesius. Among the group's themes were the extension of arts-and-crafts principles to industrial production; advocacy of a *sachlich* approach to design and production rather than a reliance on style; an emphatic stress on *quality* as the vehicle for restoring meaningful work under industrial conditions, thus alleviating the dissatisfaction with degraded goods; the establishing of a viable industrial economy; the necessity of public education and propaganda to advance this concept of quality; and all of this in the search for a harmonious culture.

The Werkbund debate of 1914 resulted from a set of theses advanced by

Muthesius for its direction.[64] His key word *Typisierung*, a word that caused such concern among some members that van de Velde offered his famous countertheses, does not appear in *Stilarchitektur*. In most interpretations of the debate, *Typisierung* has been taken to mean "standardization" in the sense of conformity to the exigencies of industrial production, and Muthesius's position in the theses has been taken to be a commitment to industrial norms at the expense of the creative power of artists or designers. It may be argued, however, that in the debate itself, neither Muthesius nor van de Velde attributed such a meaning to *Typisierung*. Rather, it meant "type," or the formulation of types or norms that could be applied to all the concerns of the Werkbund: crafts, industrial products, and architecture. For Muthesius it was a heightening of his concern for shared conventions that might provide a unified and harmonious culture. For van de Velde it represented precisely the dangers of the same phenomenon: a premature closure on creative propositions about modern culture; a false and deadening system of conventions and norms. Understood as a search for shared norms, Muthesius's position is sympathetic with his earlier stance, but it does implicitly recognize or clarify the ambiguity in his turn-of-the-century thought. How could one simultaneously honor and stress individualization as a trait of the new movement and modern times while also looking for conventions that could be the basis for a genuinely shared culture? In 1914, by advocating shared norms, Muthesius took the conservative exit from this dilemma.

ARCHITECTURE AS ART

THE THRUST OF *Stilarchitektur und Baukunst* leaves no doubt as to the disjunction of the two nouns in the title: Muthesius's advocacy is for the building-art and against style-architecture. The term *style-architecture* for him meant high style and the established architectural profession, exacerbated by too much history and the malign influence of professors of art and aesthetics. All this is seen as a characteristic product of modern urban culture, such as that proliferating in Berlin. In contrast, building-art is allied with vernacular buildings, guilds, the lower and middle classes, and humbler dwellings. Even the "art" in building-art should be understood more in its archaic sense of metier, craft, artifice.[65]

Yet Muthesius also insisted on retaining architecture's status as the Mother of the Arts. He, like many of the architects, professors, and theoreticians against whom he railed, could not help but endorse Schinkel as the last great architect practicing a unified art and architecture.[66] With "architecture as the Mother of the Arts," both the Latin root word *architectura* and the vision of the highest of the arts returned.

Perhaps a reconciliation of this with building-art would be possible. Clearly Muthesius was not describing a current state of affairs. The building-art he wished to see was yet to be won and was sought under a vision of emerging conditions of production, society, and culture. It is the asserted historical correctness of this vision of a building-art and its desired proximate realization that would win for it the right to once again be the Mother of the Arts. Furthermore, this enterprise is seen as winning art away from the rationalizing historicists and aestheticians, restoring it to its proper realm as a matter of "effects" [second edition: "feelings"], not explanation.[67] Nonetheless, there is ambiguity on this point in Muthesius's exposition—still more if one considers how this cause would be advanced within the complexities of the world. This difficulty is readily observed in Muthesius's career in these years. He was engaged with bureaucrats, politicians, industrialists, large craft producers, craftsmen, artists, architects, and critics, all of whose agendas could hardly have been aligned. Yet Muthesius could be surprised, as he was at Cologne in 1914, when one such group perceived his thought and work to be unduly weighted toward other groups.

The social vision embedded in this text must begin, as already noted, with the recognition that the idealistic socialism of Morris was of little or no political effect. Moreover, in the matters of work, craft, and product, whatever success Morris and his allies achieved had to be seen as ironically sustained by the aristocracy and the social classes created by the new industrialism. Morris found himself in the service of an elite despite himself. Additionally, industry and its products, of whatever quality, became ever more prevalent and so, too, the constrained conditions of an industrial working class who knew nothing of Morris's ideals.

A recurrent and, I think, correct commendation of the German artistic movement of the first decades of the twentieth century is that it acknowledged this defeat of Morris yet reconceived parts of his program as an experiment *within* industrial society. Muthesius played a major role in this, and *Stilarchitektur* was an early contribution. Thus we find Muthesius arguing for restoring to the worker a sense of authenticity and integrity in his production through quality in design, manufacture, and work. He believed that factory owners would be brought to such production by the pressure of an enlightened public's demand for quality.[68] Yet just as often Muthesius felt that the masses, or the public, were lacking in discrimination, thereby undermining reform and indeed supporting the negative conditions that caused his concerns.[69] German workers were said to take no notice of their rental apartments and, therefore, were unlikely agents of his envisioned reforms. The disagreeable state of German physical culture was shaped primarily by "parvenu pretension" and "sham culture."[70] In the end, Muthesius carved out the middle class and, dominantly it should seem, the lower middle class as the agents and beneficiaries of his envisioned change. Even this group would require the reformation and education that only another elite could bring: Muthesius noted with regret that the artistic German house would emerge only from a nurturing period in journals and exhibitions.[71] Later there were educational programs created by the elite figures of the Deutsche Werkbund. This was an attempt to adapt successfully to industrial culture and bring change to a much broader spectrum of the population than could be envisioned or attempted in earlier preindustrial or anti-industrial models. Nonetheless, it was also a program that did not invest trust in the classes characteristic of industrial society but rather in those of preindustrial times.

The identification and cultural investment of this middle class owed much to the historical assessments of German culture that make up the first part of *Stilarchitektur*. The Gothic was seen as the first example of a coherent Western artistic system independent of the Mediterranean and shaping the entire cultural production and everyday life of the medieval town and its burghers. It became the ultimate precedent and touchstone for a unified culture appropriate to northern societies. According to these views, the eighteenth century was the last period in which there was a commonly understood culture reaching across classes and genres, from artists through high patrons to the burgher, and from the monumental to the everyday. Muthesius was most comfortable in aligning this with the Rococo, for this was a classicism so radically transformed as to be distinctively northern, in some sense even gothicized. Nonetheless (and somewhat more strongly in the second edition), Muthesius, like other architects and critics, could also recognize these traits in the simplified classicism around 1800—in the work of Schinkel but preferably in the generalized and often anonymous work of the Biedermeier period from 1815 to 1848.

Despite the restrictions imposed by imitation, the Gothic revival in England initiated the reassertion of northern cultural values according to Muthesius. It opened doors that yielded the success of the new architecture. The very possibility of these exemplars offered for consideration by Muthesius was owing to a middle class free of Italianate pretensions: the argument is that classicism insists on its universality and eternal standards and thus also embraces formalism and imitation. In contrast the variant northern periods are "an expression of the inner nature . . . of contemporary developments";[72] they are individual and recognize "that there can be only one standard for art, namely that which expresses the life and culture of the time."[73] For Muthesius it was a distinctively northern and even particularly Germanic (or as he prefers, Nordic) opportunity to realize a historically justified reform through an empowered middle class enjoying a freedom of taste. For him this individualistic German conception of art is what can, in the best sense, be designated as "modern."[74] It is not surprising, then, that we find Muthesius led into increasingly nationalistic, and finally chauvinistic, regard for the German middle class to whom he addresses his message and from whom he expects so much. With the claim that the ascendant new art was created basically by Germanic peoples, he observes the decline of the Latin peoples and their arts,[75] and asserts:

> If we restrict ourselves to the homegrown, and if each of us impartially follows his own individual artistic inclinations, then we will soon have not only a reasonable but also a national, vernacular building-art. Nationality in art need not be artificially bred. If one raises genuine people, we will have a genuine art that for every individual with a sincere character can be nothing other than national. For every genuine person is a part of a genuine nationality.[76]

He expanded on this concept in the second edition of *Stilarchitektur*.

> As the bearer of the new ideas, a new spiritual aristocracy arises, which this time stems from the best of the middle class rather than the hereditary aristocratic elements, and this especially clearly signals the new and enlarged goal of the movement: the creation of a contemporary middle-class art. A strong artistic current, unimaginable ten years ago, streams through the German heart, and a deep desire for a purer state of art moves the whole of Germany.[77]

It is also this wholehearted embrace of the middle class as the agent and the destination of the new art that leads Muthesius, despite a more general set of assumptions, to a unique focus on the single-family house. Notwithstanding that the common dwelling in Germany of his time was the rental apartment; notwithstanding his own opinion that the culture of the house was still little developed in Germany; notwithstanding his regret that not even the wealthy often enough sought out the comforts of the villa, still Muthesius draws the conclusion that "a change in our German artistic situation can only take its start in the German house," adding "which essentially is yet to be created."[78]

It would appear that Muthesius polemically underestimated the appeal of the single-family house for the Germans of his own day and the following decades, but it was this emphasis that prevented Muthesius's architectural thinking from engaging the problems and potentials of housing the greater number or of rethinking the industrial city.

On the other hand, a matter that was only an aside for Muthesius, but of which he was critical and prescient, was that of the restoration of ancient—in this case mainly medieval—buildings. He was keen in recognizing the obvious modernity, and soon even the ability to recognize a history within this modernity, of the manners of "restoring" old buildings. Recognizing that such works are documents better known in a ruinous state than in a ruined reworking, he preferred a halt to all restoration.[79]

CONCLUSION

MUTHESIUS'S INORDINATE EMPHASIS on the house and middle-class culture, his nationalism and chauvinism, his neglect of social housing and the city— all these matters give pause and distance one from his position. Nonetheless, these aspects of his argument are not intrinsic to his fundamental program. That program centers on the concept of *sachliche Kunst*, which in this context might be termed "a realist architecture," the posited extension and transformation of pure *Sachlichkeit* to the full range of architectural production. That Muthesius focuses that extension almost wholly on the house does not limit the generality of the argument; it could be directed to housing, to civic institutions, to the city.

We can now draw some conclusions from this and other material.[80] It was commonplace to recognize the engineering achievements of the nineteenth century, from tools or instruments to the great bridges and railroad sheds. Whether the critics saw these works as exemplary achievements or, resignedly, as the representative objects of a materialist epoch, they agreed that such works and the processes that produced them were marked by rationality, functionalism, and the direct satisfaction of need. Muthesius subsumed such qualities under the term "pure" *Sachlichkeit*. Other authors, at least in speaking of architecture, gave the term *Sachlichkeit* further extension, incorporating within it the needs to be satisfied, the demands of local atmosphere or milieu, recognizing that an arbitrariness of formal invention is not eliminated even if one recognizes the constraints within which it operates. Muthesius was, after all, in accord with this move when he distinguished between pure *Sachlichkeit* and a *sachlich*, or realist, art and architecture.[81]

Sachlichkeit is, then, a convenient umbrella term that invokes simplicity, a rational and straightforward attention to needs as well as to materials and processes. In the realm of art and architecture, at least at the turn of the twentieth century, the range of needs was extended, however, and in such a way that none of these authors would expect a calculus of their realist architecture. A realist architecture imposes certain desiderata and constraints, but it still requires conventions or inventions that are not to be incorporated by a mechanical processing of a unique stipulation of needs.[82]

Reason is imperative, but reason that is guided by our affections. *Sachliche Kunst*, a realist architecture, unlike the positivism of pure *Sachlichkeit*, is realism that points to interaction between the actor and the world—a theoretical position descending from inquiries into the sources of knowledge conducted in England and Germany around 1800. Whether by received custom or by our challenges to received conventions, we frame the conditions of our knowing and our existence—accepting, with Clifford Geertz, the view of Max Weber: we spin the webs of our own understanding.[83] Denying any certainty to this web, to this framework, relishing its hypothetical character, we can entertain its metaphysical propositions as much as its material implications.

A realist architecture mistrusts universalist claims, such as those voiced by the Darmstadt Artists' Colony, in which art and the great artist magnanimously were to impose forms that would dictate to life. A realist architecture rejects a necessary, organic relation of cultural production to blood and soil (even if this claim is clearer in the thought of Loos than in that of Muthesius). Realist architecture respects but subsumes the pure *Sachlichkeit* of the calculation of mechanical needs. It establishes a condition of knowing and association that cannot maintain its balance without speculative innovation; but this too will ordinarily appear within a framework that is the fruit of earlier speculations. Within a realist architecture there is an impetus to understand and use our received condition as much as to criticize and change it.

I would not like to end this introduction without recognizing certain dangers into which this program of realist architecture may slide. While it is one of the strengths of this type of architecture to concern itself with the cultural life of its generation, one is thereby also implicated in that cultural life. A *sachlich* search of this cultural life may incline one to take the status quo as a given. Certain forms or conventions may not be raised to consciousness. Others may be accepted or even "realistically" endorsed simply because they are there. Thus can emerge the uncritical appreciation of anonymous or vernacular forms of a place or of the social as well as physical conventions of that place. Still more problematically these concerns may be employed to pose a nostalgic and, finally, a coercive program of a rooted, totalizing culture. The definition and appreciation of regional differences can escalate into nationalism and, finally, into racism. Muthesius's formulations contained this evident nationalism, which he employed to resist French influence, to delimit even that which might be learned from his much-studied English works, and to impel a chauvinist dimension within his program for the German arts. Still more emphatic commitments to the invention of a rooted German culture were briefly mentioned at the beginning of this essay, and indeed such efforts were part of a broad and sustained program in the architectural culture of Germany before and after 1900. The name of Paul Schultze-Naumburg may suffice to evidence the possible transition from an inquiry into local architectural culture to a racist program.[84] It is this problematic aspect of German architecture to which Francesco Dal Co gives valuable and concerted attention—and also rightly notes the close ties between these appeals to rootedness and the ambitions for a true *Wohnkultur*, or culture of dwelling.[85] Yet, I think it is correct to note that the form of *Wohnkultur* that one may recognize in the advocacy of Meier-Graefe, in Loos, and in the best of Muthesius's work is both critical and projective, making no appeal to rootedness but rather to an interactive transformation of both architecture and social and cultural life.

It is possible, I think, to identify where the faulted programs transgress the position advanced as *sachliche Kunst*, or realist architecture. As opposed to pure *Sachlichkeit,* I would argue that a strength of *sachliche Kunst* is its acceptance, but properly a critical acceptance, of a cultural setting as a necessary and enabling condition for its realist inquiry. This is the acceptance of a metaphysic, of certain speculations, of an arbitrariness at the very beginning of the inquiry. To avoid the slide from this critical acceptance of convention to an acceptance of the status quo, or still more problematically to positions of nationalism and racism, it is imperative that one does not lose sight of the arbitrary basis of conventions—that they be weighed in the light of alternatives and innovations, be as much the focus of criticism as of exposition. Here is the crucial difference between the work of Loos and that of Schultze-Naumburg or, less dramatically, even between Loos and Muthesius.

NOTES

References of the type "*Style-Architecture and Building-Art* [56]" direct the reader to the appropriate page of the translation of Muthesius's text that appears in this volume. The translation is based on the first edition of 1902, which appears in bold type. Additions made to the second edition of 1903 appear in nonbold type. The use of a typographic device—a dotted underscore—and explanations in the accompanying endnotes indicate variants between the 1902 and 1903 editions of Muthesius's text. Indications of variants are only furnished in the Introduction when they are relevant to the discussion.

1. Hermann Muthesius, *Stilarchitektur und Baukunst: Wandlungen der Architektur im XIX. Jahrhundert und ihr heutiger Standpunkt* (Mülheim an der Ruhr: K. Schimmelpfeng, 1902; 2nd ed., Mülheim an der Ruhr: K. Schimmelpfeng, 1903). The second edition was subtitled *Wandlungen der Architektur und der gewerblichen Künste im neunzehnten Jahrhundert und ihr heutiger Standpunkt.*

2. The biographical data in this section are from Wiltrud Petsch-Bahr, "Hermann Muthesius," in Wolfgang Ribbe and Wolfgang Schäche, eds., *Baumeister, Architekten, Stadtplaner: Biographien zur baulichen Entwicklung Berlins* (Berlin: Stapp, 1987), 321–40.

3. Hermann Muthesius, *Italienische Reise-Eindrücke* (Berlin: W. Ernst & Sohn, 1898), 51–52.

4. The three publications are: *Die englische Baukunst der Gegenwart: Beispiele neuer englischer Profanbauten* (Leipzig: Cosmoz, 1900); *Die neuere kirchliche Baukunst in England: Entwicklung, Bedingungen und Grundzüge des Kirchenbaues der englischen Staatskirche und der Secten* (Berlin: W. Ernst & Sohn, 1901); and *Das englische Haus: Entwicklung, Bedingungen, Anlage, Aufbau, Einrichtung und Innenraum,* 3 vols. (Berlin: Ernst Wasmuth, 1904–1905; 2nd ed., Berlin: Ernst Wasmuth, 1908–1911; one vol. English ed., New York: Rizzoli, 1979).

5. See Hans Joachim Hubrich, *Hermann Muthesius: Die Schriften zu Architektur, Kunstgewerbe, Industrie in der "Neuen Bewegung"* (Berlin: Mann, 1981).

6. A convenient compendium of Muthesius's architecture is Silvano Custoza, Maurizio Vogliazzo, and Julius Posener, *Muthesius* (Milan: Electa, 1981). Julius Posener is a major interpreter of Muthesius, both in English and German. See his "Muthesius," *Architects Year Book* 10 (1962): 45–51; *From Schinkel to the Bauhaus* (London: The Architectural Association, 1972); "Muthesius als Architekt," *Werkbundarchiv* 1 (1972): 55–80; "Muthesius as Architect," *Lotus* 9 (Feb. 1975): 104–15; and, with Sonja Günther, eds., *Hermann Muthesius, 1861–1927* (Berlin: Akademie der Künste, 1977). See also Stefan Muthesius, *Das englische Vorbild: Eine Studie zu den deutschen Reformbewegungen in Architektur, Wohnbau und Kunstgewerbe im späteren 19. Jahrhundert* (Munich: Prestel, 1974); and Wiltrud Petsch-Bahr (see note 2).

7. Hermann Muthesius, *Wie baue ich mein Haus?* (Munich: F. Bruckmann, 1917). A second, revised and enlarged, edition in the same year—less elegantly produced—gave more consideration to modest houses.

8. Hermann Muthesius, *Kann ich auch jetzt noch mein Haus bauen? Richtlinien für den wirklich sparsamen Bau des bürgerlichen Einfamilienhauses . . . Mit Beispielen* (Munich: F. Bruckmann, 1920).

9. Johann Joachim Winckelmann, *Geschichte der Kunst des Altertums* (Dresden: Walther, 1764).

10. The concepts embodied in the word *Sachlichkeit* are central to Muthesius's argument in *Stilarchitektur. Sachlichkeit* is often translated as "objectivity" or "reality." It and its adjectival form, *sachlich*, may also connote the "functional," "practical," "pragmatic," "material," "factual," "matter-of-fact," "artless," and "straightforward." In almost any German context a single English word cannot provide an adequate translation. Additionally, the intended meaning has shifted with different authors and in different periods of the nineteenth- and twentieth-century discourse on art and architecture. This Introduction attempts to build a nuanced view of the use of this word at the turn of the century. As it is introduced in the first part of the essay, what seems to be the most adequate English translation is offered. When *Sachlichkeit* appears in Muthesius's advocacy, I have usually translated it as "straightforwardness," both for the similarity of construction and because this term properly avoids the too demanding claims of "objectivity" (for Muthesius, *"reine* [pure] *Sachlichkeit"*) and the too narrow and too worn connotations of "practicality" or "functionalism." As the argument of the Introduction unfolds, the more complex connotations are assumed to be developed and clarified through context and the German word is presented without translation. The argument can be anticipated by referring to pp. 34–35 of this Introduction.

11. The material in this paragraph is drawn from the essay "Vom Nutzen und Nachteil der Historie für das Leben" (The use and abuse of history), which first appeared in 1874 in Friedrich Wilhelm Nietzsche's *Unzeitgemässe Betrachtungen,* translated into English as *Thoughts out of Season* (New York: Liberal Arts Press, 1949), 73–75; and more recently as *Unmodern Observations* (New Haven: Yale, 1990), 87ff.

12. See, for example Henry van de Velde, *Laienpredigten* (Leipzig: Seemann, 1902), 16. The influence of Nietzsche in the revolutionary art movement in Belgium around 1890 is specifically mentioned. Van de Velde later designed the Nietzsche-Archiv in Weimar (1903).

13. [Julius Langbehn], *Rembrandt als Erzieher, von einem Deutschen* (Leipzig: Hirschfeld, 1890).

14. Hermann Muthesius, *Kultur und Kunst: Gesammelte Aufsätze über künstlerische Fragen der Gegenwart* (Jena: E. Diederichs, 1904; reprint, Nendeln: Kraus, 1976).

15. Konrad Lange's *Die künstlerische Erziehung der deutschen Jugend* (Darmstadt: Bergstrasser, 1893) was a book of related significance, influenced by Langbehn; it urged an artistic education for all German children.

An early enthusiast for feeling and the "heart" as opposed to reason and the mind was Heinrich Pudor, a constant advocate of the movement in the arts discussed here. See, for example, his *Die Welt als Musik* (Dresden: Albanus, n.d. [a lecture given in 1891]), and *Kaiser Wilhelm II und Rembrandt als Erzieher* (2nd enlarged ed., Dresden: O. Damm, 1891).

In his *Der Weg der Kunst* (Jena: Diederichs, 1904), Albert Dresdner draws upon Nietzsche and Langbehn to put his case against modern science, Impressionism, and the corset, and in favor of the dance, artistic education, etc. Both this work and Muthesius's *Kultur und Kunst* were published by Eugen Diederichs, as were a series of related volumes by Ludwig von Kunowski. Diederichs could, and did, write prospectuses for his press, which, in leading from one of his publications to the next, formed not just an essay but a coherent program for cultural reform. Some of his authors might cite Langbehn favorably, but the total program was broader. Diederichs considered himself the leading publisher of what was termed the *Neuromantik*. Under this term were grouped those artists, poets, essayists, historians, and philosophers who sought a comprehensive view of life such as that pursued by the early nineteenth-century Romantics. Goethe may be mentioned as one of the great models, but there were others, too, and of other eras: for example, Paracelsus and Albrecht Dürer. Diederichs felt that this admirable desire for an adequate *Naturphilosophie* had been lost in the materialism, naturalism, and specialization of the latter nineteenth century. See, for example, Diederichs's program for his press in 1900, which appears in Lulu von Strauss and Torney-Diederichs, ed., *Eugen Diederichs: Leben und Werk* (Jena: E. Diederichs, 1936), 52–53.

For an excellent consideration of Langbehn and other strongly nationalistic ideologists, see Fritz Stern, *The Politics of Cultural Despair: A Study in the Rise of the Germanic Ideology* (Berkeley: Univ. of California Press, 1961).

16. Stefan Muthesius, "Deutschland unter englischen Einfluss, 1880–1897," in idem, *Das englische Vorbild* (Munich: Prestel, 1974), 96–118.

17. Robert Dohme, *Das englische Haus: Eine kultur- und baugeschichtliche Skizze* (Braunschweig: G. Westermann, 1888).

18. Ibid., 42.

19. Inigo Jones (1573–1652), English architect.

20. *Style-Architecture and Building-Art* [66].

21. See *Style-Architecture and Building-Art* [66]. See also the monograph by Anthony Quiney, *John Loughborough Pearson* (New Haven: Yale Univ. Press, 1979).

22. *Style-Architecture and Building-Art* [67].

23. *Style-Architecture and Building-Art* [96–97].

24. After an international competition in 1851, Friedrich Bürklein (1813–1872), the favored architect of King Maximilian II of Bavaria, was charged with conceiving a new architectural style to be demonstrated in the Maximilianstrasse, an eastward extension from the old city of Munich. The enterprise was conducted under criticism that new styles were not "made" but developed. See Gerhard Hojer, "München—Maximilianstrasse und Maximilianstil," in Ludwig Grote, ed., *Die Deutsche Stadt im 19. Jahrhundert* (Munich: Prestel, 1974), 33–65; and,

in a more general context, Klaus Döhmer, *"In welchem Style sollen wir bauen?": Architektur-theorie zwischen Klassizismus und Jugendstil* (Munich: Prestel, 1976).

25. *Style-Architecture and Building-Art* [98].

26. *Style-Architecture and Building-Art* [87].

27. *Style-Architecture and Building-Art* [95].

28. *Style-Architecture and Building-Art* [89].

29. *Style-Architecture and Building-Art* [90–91].

30. *Style-Architecture and Building-Art* [97].

31. *Style-Architecture and Building-Art* [50].

32. *Style-Architecture and Building-Art* [50].

33. *Style-Architecture and Building-Art* [98].

34. *Style-Architecture and Building-Art* [80].

35. *Style-Architecture and Building-Art* [98].

36. Julius Meier-Graefe, "Ein modernes Milieu," *Dekorative Kunst* 4–8, no. 7 (April 1901): 261.

37. Hermann Muthesius, "Neues Ornament und neue Kunst," *Dekorative Kunst* 4–8, no. 9 (June 1901): 364–66: ". . . *dieses Beispieles, das fast alle die Ideale einer echten neuen Kunst zu verwirklichen scheint und in seiner schlichten Behaglichkeit und ornamentlosen Grösse eine wahre Erquickung bedeutet.*"

38. Richard Streiter, "Aus München," *Pan*, no. 3 (1896): 249; also in idem, *Ausgewählte Schriften zur Aesthetik und Kunst-Geschichte* (Munich: Delphin, 1913), 32: "*Realismus in der Architektur, das ist die weitgehendste Berücksichtigung der realen Werdebedingungen eines Bau-werks, die möglichst vollkommene Erfüllung der Forderungen der Zweckmässigkeit, Bequemlich-keit, Gesundheitsförderlichkeit, mit einem Wort: die Sachlichkeit. Aber das ist noch nicht alles. Wie der Realismus der Dichtung als eine seiner Hauptaufgaben es betrachtet, den Zusammenhang der Charaktere mit ihrem Milieu scharf ins Auge zu fassen, so sieht die verwandte Richtung in der Architektur ein vor allem erstrebenswertes Ziel künstlerischer Wahrhaftigkeit darin den Charakter eines Bauwerkes nicht aus seiner Zweckbestimmung allein, sondern auch aus dem Milieu, aus der Eigenart der jeweilig vorhandenen Baustoffe, aus der Landschaftlich und geschichtlich bedingten Stimmung der Oertlichkeit heraus zu entwickeln.*"

39. Stanford Anderson, "Sachlichkeit and Modernity, or Realist Architecture," in Harry Francis Mallgrave, ed., *Otto Wagner: Reflections on the Raiment of Modernity* (Santa Monica: The Getty Center for the History of Art and the Humanities, 1993), 339.

40. *Style-Architecture and Building-Art* [85].

41. *Style-Architecture and Building-Art* [96].

42. *Style-Architecture and Building-Art* [94].

43. *Style-Architecture and Building-Art* [93].

44. *Style-Architecture and Building-Art* [48, 53].

45. *Style-Architecture and Building-Art* [81].

46. *Style-Architecture and Building-Art* [99], emphasis mine.

47. The date on the cover of the first edition is 1901, but 1902 appears on the title page.

48. *Style-Architecture and Building-Art* [47]. All quotations in this paragraph are taken from the second paragraph of Muthesius's foreword to the second edition.

49. *Style-Architecture and Building-Art* [50].

50. *Style-Architecture and Building-Art* [97].

51. *Style-Architecture and Building-Art* [53].

52. *Style-Architecture and Building-Art* [85–91].

53. This paragraph summarizes an addition to the second edition of *Style-Architecture and Building-Art* [91–96].

54. *Style-Architecture and Building-Art* [94].

55. Joseph August Lux, "Stilarchitektur und Baukunst," *Der Architekt* 8 (1902): 45–47.

56. William R. Lethaby, *Form in Civilization: Collected Papers on Art and Labour* (London: Oxford Univ. Press, 1922; 2nd. ed., 1957).

57. William R. Lethaby, "Modern German Architecture and What We May Learn from It," in idem (see note 56), 96–105.

58. *Style-Architecture and Building-Art* [82].

59. Meier-Graefe (see note 36), 264: "*Die Bewegung wird wahrscheinlich und hoffentlich den Schröder'schen Weg gehen; . . . Die Wiener fangen schon an, Loos macht ostentativ in Wien Möbel ohne jedes Ornament und bleibt nicht ohne Einfluss.*" For his part, Muthesius sustained his call for artistic production devoid of artfulness: in his *Kunstgewerbe und Architektur* (Jena: Diederichs, 1907), Muthesius ends the chapter titled "Das Moderne in der Architektur" with the words of Hamlet's mother to Polonius: "More matter with less art."

60. Adolf Loos, *Ins Leere gesprochen, 1897–1900* (Paris: Crès, 1921; reprint, Vienna: G. Prachner, 1981). Translated by Jane O. Newman and John H. Smith as *Spoken into the Void: Collected Essays, 1897–1900* (Cambridge, Mass.: MIT Press, 1982).

61. This was overtly manifest in 1907 when Muthesius played a lead role in the establishment of the Deutsche Werkbund while Loos quickly dismissed this enterprise for making the error of the Jugendstil again: the overarching definition of form for all scales of production by an elite of artist-designers. See Adolf Loos, "Die Überflüssigen (Deutscher Werkbund)" (1908), in *Trotzdem, 1900–1930* (Innsbruck: Brenner, 1931; reprint, Vienna: G. Prachner, 1982), 71–73.

More generally, despite his attention to English domestic architecture, Muthesius was concertedly nationalist, polemicizing a distinctly German artistic production. Loos was critical of the Viennese situation, honing his arguments by international awareness and advocating the acceptance of certain foreign innovations. I have elsewhere argued that Loos's thought and production, being more consistent and more critical as well as more innovative, would provide the preferred basis for a characterization and evaluation of a program of realist architecture.

62. Richard Streiter, *Architektonische Zeitfragen: Eine Sammlung und Sichtung verschiedener Anschauungen mit besonderer Beziehung auf Professor Otto Wagners Schrift "Moderne Architektur"* (1898), in idem, 1913 (see note 38), 55–149 and the notes on 325–27. See also the essays by J. Duncan Berry, Harry Mallgrave, and Stanford Anderson in Mallgrave (see note 39).

63. Joan Campbell, *The German Werkbund: The Politics of Reform in the Applied Arts* (Princeton: Princeton Univ. Press, 1978); and Kurt Junghanns, *Der Deutsche Werkbund: Sein erstes Jahrzehnt* (Berlin: Henschel, 1982).

64. See Stanford Anderson, "Deutscher Werkbund—the 1914 Debate: Hermann Muthesius versus Henry van de Velde," in Ben Farmer and Hentie Louw, eds., *Companion to Contemporary Architectural Thought* (London: Routledge, 1993), 462–67.

65. Muthesius's polarization of "style-architecture" versus "building-art" required a gross simplification, a polemically narrow interpretation of nineteenth-century architectural thought and practice. This combative position, understandable in a small tract, came to characterize much of the criticism and historiography of modern architecture until the last third of the twentieth century.

66. *Style-Architecture and Building-Art* [54–55].

67. *Style-Architecture and Building-Art* [56].

68. *Style-Architecture and Building-Art* [92].

69. *Style-Architecture and Building-Art* [87].

70. *Style-Architecture and Building-Art* [89].

71. *Style-Architecture and Building-Art* [96–97].

72. *Style-Architecture and Building-Art* [76].

73. *Style-Architecture and Building-Art* [61].

74. *Style-Architecture and Building-Art* [99].

75. *Style-Architecture and Building-Art* [76–77].

76. *Style-Architecture and Building-Art* [97].

77. *Style-Architecture and Building-Art* [100].

78. *Style-Architecture and Building-Art* [85].

79. *Style-Architecture and Building-Art* [63–64]. See also Hermann Muthesius, "Die 'Wiederherstellung' unserer alten Bauten," in idem, 1904 (see note 14), 117–55.

80. This concluding material is modified from Anderson (see note 39).

81. With the term *realist art*, I do not intend to subsume all other uses of that term, from nineteenth-century French painting to socialist realism, but rather to avail myself of an English term, here used with specific reference to the concept discussed in this essay.

82. A similar interpretation of architecture may already be recognized in Arthur Schopenhauer, *The World as Will and Representation,* trans. E. F. J. Payne (Indian Hills, Colo.: Falcon's Wing Press, 1958; reprint, New York: Dover, 1969), esp. vol. 1, sec. 43.

83. Clifford Geertz, *The Interpretation of Culture* (New York: Basic Books, 1973), 5.

84. Barbara Miller Lane, *Architecture and Politics in Germany, 1918–1945* (Cambridge, Mass.: Harvard Univ. Press, 1968), esp. 133ff.

85. Francesco Dal Co, *Figures of Architecture and Thought: German Architecture Culture, 1880–1920* (New York: Rizzoli, 1990). See especially the chapter "Culture of Dwelling."

STYLE-ARCHITECTURE AND BUILDING-ART:
TRANSFORMATIONS OF ARCHITECTURE IN THE NINETEENTH CENTURY AND ITS PRESENT CONDITION[1]

The translation that follows is based on the first edition of Muthesius's *Stilarchitektur und Baukunst* (1902). The first edition text is rendered in a bold typeface. Textual additions that were made to the second edition of 1903 are indicated by use of non-bold type. A dotted underscore has been used to indicate either deletions or variations that occur in the second edition. Changes marked with the dotted underscore are explained more fully in notes that follow the translation.

—S. A.

FOREWORD
{to the second edition}

That, contrary to expectations, the sale of the first edition quickly made a second necessary is encouraging above all for this reason: it indicates that the time nears in which architectural questions will also be considered in wider circles. The word *architecture* has, until recently, had a repelling effect upon the public—akin to a jet of cold water; a book whose title bore the word *architecture* was seen as a professional work, of no interest to anyone beyond this narrow circle.

The artistic movement in whose center we stand began with the applied arts. It was these that again directed the public's attention to tectonic questions. One indication of this is our flourishing journalism in the field of the wrongly termed "decorative art." Contemporary artistic issues are not, however, settled with embroidered sofa pillows, or even with artistic interiors. As long as we live in the midst of the barbarism of ashlar, stucco, and brick that propagates in our streets and suburbs and even begins to desolate our towns, we are far removed from the artistic liberation for which the time appears to yearn. The central issue of the new artistic movement is architecture.

Compared to the first edition, which basically conveyed two lectures given in the winter of 1901, this second edition is significantly enlarged, particularly by a supplement on the condition of the arts and crafts. At the same time, the publisher has responded to the often expressed wish to set the price of the book sufficiently low so that it can reach wider circles.

—Hermann Muthesius
Nikolassee b. Wannsee
August 1903

FOR MY BROTHER KARL[2]

INDEED, I HAVE A HOPE THAT IT WILL
BE FROM SUCH NECESSARY, UNPRE-
TENTIOUS BUILDINGS THAT THE
NEW AND GENUINE ARCHITECTURE
WILL SPRING, RATHER THAN FROM
OUR EXPERIMENTS IN CONSCIOUS
STYLE MORE OR LESS AMBITIOUS, OR
THOSE FOR WHICH THE IMMORTAL
DICKENS HAS GIVEN US THE NEVER-
TO-BE-FORGOTTEN ADJECTIVE
"ARCHITECTOORALOORAL."[3]

—William Morris

I

Today there is general agreement that architecture is the least understood of all the arts, the art to which people bring the most diminished interest. Indeed, in Germany today it is seriously contested whether architecture is an art at all, whether the architect is an artist or not. The old truth, valid in all epochs, that architecture is the Mother of the Arts, that all the plastic arts (painting, sculpture, and the various applied arts) are dependent on architecture and, as it were, march under her leadership—this truth today sounds like a fairy tale. Yet we have only to recall the great flowerings of the building-art—Greek, Roman, and Gothic times—to observe that this truth was in those times so self-evident that no one needed to express it. The entire plastic art of those times stood under the sign of architecture. One may say: art was architecture. Painting was a mural in the service of an architectural concept; sculpture was the ornament of architecture, like the precious stone that decorates the golden crown; the applied arts—that is, in those times, handicrafts—were naturally part of architecture.

That this has become so very different today—indeed, that this timeless, fundamental relationship among the plastic arts seems so utterly strange is itself the best indication of the artificial conditions under which our contemporary artistic life stirs. Our plastic art has lost its footing; it hovers, so to speak, in the air. Painting and sculpture today lack that defined impulse that compels them to acknowledge their dependence on architecture; the controlling decorative rule that prevailed into[5] the early Renaissance is lost. These arts have more or less become anecdotal, and today it is the anecdote almost alone that maintains the public's interest in the arts. The minor arts, even with the happy impulse they had[6] received in Germany at the end of the nineteenth century, spin helplessly this way and that, and will do so as long as the refuge of the great Mother Architecture—in this case the artistic[7] dwelling— is lacking.

THE
NINETEENTH
CENTURY
AND ART

This question can best be answered by glancing back to the path that architecture traveled in its most recent development, especially in the nineteenth century.

As we crossed the threshold of the new century, we were not lacking in reflections that sought to capture in a few words the significance of the passing century. The nineteenth century was termed the century of transportation, of electricity, of the natural sciences, of historical research, the century of the national armies, of labor, of machines. Each of these labels is of little value, but taken collectively we notice that no one has dared to call the nineteenth century the century of art. Every acclaimed accomplishment is scientific in nature—those that devolve from the intellectual activity of mankind. Nothing is said of the arts; they obviously played no role in the nineteenth century. And indeed in this century every field was forcefully reshaped: the civilized world has been overtaken[8] with a desire for practical application, with earnestness for the comprehension of life, and with a compulsion for research and acquisition that were unknown in earlier times. This activity was, however, very one-sided: purely intellectual or technically oriented. Yet with regard to art, especially the plastic arts, we can think of no better way to designate[9] this period than as the "inartistic century."

EARLIER
ARTISTIC
PERIODS

In judging the question of whether a period can be termed artistic or inartistic, no factor is so decisive as the degree to which art is the property of the entire people— to what extent it is an essential part of the cultural endowment of the time. In this sense, as a visit to our ethnological museums will demonstrate, almost all aboriginal tribes must be termed artistic, for the first human activity, as evidenced in the production of weapons and implements, is rarely, even among the most primitive of peoples, separable from artistic activity. This shows us that the artistic instinct belongs to the elementary powers of mankind and casts a still more peculiar light on a time such as ours, which has left these powers to wither.

Since the beginning of history, two luminous periods stand out in Western culture as notably artistic: Greek antiquity and the Nordic Middle Ages. The first denotes an artistic height that the world can hardly hope again to attain; the second, at the very least, embodies that complete artistic independence and that absolute artistic ethnicity that are basic conditions of any artistic era. Greek art was so powerful, so triumphant, and so superior that not only did the entire culture of its homeland stand under its influence, but it also nurtured the mighty Roman Empire—itself artistically infertile.

GREEK ART

Gothic art, while not wholly independent of antiquity, is nevertheless a completely independent cultural manifestation and is the only original art, in addition to the Greek, to develop in the Western cultural[10] world. If the whole of antiquity was dependent on Greek art, Gothic art provides the artistic roots of a new time; it is the art of the Nordic peoples, from which there developed in the first Gothic golden age that glorious early harvest of architecture and its related arts. The Gothic Middle Ages represented the first triumph of an art fundamentally different from classical art, an art fully developed, unified in all its manifestations, infusing every production of the human hand, and, above all, ethnic in the best sense. It was, therefore, in its own way a perfect period of art.

GOTHIC

Like everything in the world, Gothic art was subject to change and transformation. There came the time when the antique world, whose spirit forcefully survived even its physical decline, brought new artistic ideals to the north. The age of humanism in the liberal arts—of the Renaissance in the fine arts—ascended, and led to a flowering of the arts, particularly in painting and sculpture. This was not equally true for architecture. Whereas in painting, and in a certain sense also in sculpture, these new influences assisted in bringing an extant youthfulness to maturity, in architecture a fully developed art was rudely broken and a rich artistic tradition was cast aside. What was achieved in Renaissance building-art could be but a pale image of a superior original art—a claim that will be evident to every visitor to Italy who observes how any single antique building (the Roman Colosseum or the Pantheon, for example) eclipses the entire building-art of the Renaissance.

THE FIRST ARTISTIC REVOLUTION

Yet another determining factor for art was born in that time. The Renaissance wrought a division in the largely stable social classes of the Middle Ages. It introduced the concept of the "cultured"—those adepts in the classical languages who from this period forward collectively represented the spiritual elect of the people, and who held themselves as a special social class above the ethnic substratum of the nation. The new art was also allied to this class. Henceforth, an art for the ruling class replaced the Gothic art of the people.[11] The fate of art now rested with the upper classes; the wealthy and educated art patron engaged the artist.

Since this new spirit imposed itself relatively slowly, and since the admirable guild spirit of that time robustly assimilated the new, this nascent artistic movement did not have the unhealthy influence on the craftsmen, artisans, and the entire work force of the architects that one might have anticipated in the breakdown of all formal traditions. Even the strong character of the Gothic works made its contribution, since it provided the newly introduced artistic forms with an excellent schooling, one in which the artificially grafted Renaissance art could prosper. Yet painting and sculpture, effecting the first artistic revolution of our culture, seized the occasion to make themselves independent. Painting, in particular, traveled a path independent of architecture; it tended toward the minor specialization of panel painting, which it subsequently emphasized and fully exhausted. In this, painting so dominated the field that for the average person today the concept of art is synonymous with oil painting on canvas.

THE
EIGHTEENTH
CENTURY During the Renaissance, architecture vacillated between a kind of autonomous development of grafted forms and a closer imitation of the old mother art of antiquity. Around the middle of the eighteenth century there was the greatest deviation from the latter position, as a virtually novel, amiably cheerful, and light art that breathed the joy of life was sought—the so-called Rococo. If, according to the viewpoint previously advanced, we consider this art in terms of its unity and the degree to which it was a common cultural property, then we must value it highly. It not only mirrored the life of the time perfectly but also fully imbued—as in the case of the Gothic— all the contemporary expressions of life. The imported antique forms appeared to be fully assimilated; a marriage of the classical spirit with that of the time seemed to have been achieved. From the tobacco box of the simple burgher to the most refined furniture of the princely interior, from the facade of the house of the small-town burgher to the splendid Jesuit church, we have a completely unified cultural model before us. Painting, sculpture, and architecture breathed the same spirit. Above all, every artisan was so at home with the formal language of the time that it appeared to him as truly the natural means of expression, the correctness of which no one doubted. Moreover, every artisan and craftsman practiced this formal language so perfectly that the most commonplace craft products appear to us today as works of art, worthy to be placed in our museums or to adorn the collector's cabinet. Architecture was still dominant, if not as all powerful as in Gothic times. The achieve-

ments of the master mason were so fine and assured that the buildings, even in their ultimate variations, still refresh us. When we now look back on that time, it appears to us, from an artistic standpoint, as altogether paradisal.[12]

The eighteenth century concluded this amalgamating process, which had been introduced into the Nordic lands with the penetration of antique influences. Though the dominant art was outspokenly aristocratic, the aristocracy, nevertheless, had such a steady and decisive influence on the broader practice of the applied arts through two centuries that the cultural image again became unified. Yet taking place alongside this was a more important event. From high aristocratic art the middle class drew an art for its own needs—simple, matter-of-fact [*sachlich*],[13] and reasonable, which shared with aristocratic art only the forms derived from antiquity, not the pomp and need for representation. A stroll through the streets of almost any German town still reveals numerous examples of this admirable architecture of the burghers of the eighteenth century, which still could serve as a model for our contemporary conditions. Unfortunately they have not yet been sufficiently taken into consideration. In their simplicity, they impress us too little and appear too self-effacing in relation to aristocratic art. A hundred years later it was the aristocratic art—not the architecture of the burghers—that was imitated as architects replicated the styles chronologically. And the aristocratic influence was, moreover, the worst. The bourgeoisie were now so parvenu, so lacking in judgment and backbone, that they grasped this aristocratic art with covetous hands and created those monstrosities of artificial splendor and false luster, those now impertinent, overladen stucco facades of urban streets and the pompous and shabby appointments of our rental dwellings. Compared to this evidence of modern culture, the perfected artistic period of the eighteenth century can only appear to us as altogether paradisal.[14]

MIDDLE-CLASS ART

Also during that period a tendency emerged under whose sign all subsequent artistic development would stand, and which gave to the art of the next century its particular character. Emerging as a reaction against the earlier, lighthearted spirit of the times, one sought a purity and simplicity that expressed itself artistically in returning to the then newly discovered Greek antiquity. The work on the antiquities of Athens by the English architects Stuart and Revett, which appeared in 1762, forms the milestone of this new discovery.[15]

THE SECOND ARTISTIC REVOLUTION

The upheaval in artistic views that took place, the enthusiasm with which one celebrated a new ideal, was immense. Everyone at the time had the feeling that now, after a long period of gloom, the sun of artistic knowledge was ascending—that this sun would enlighten a new, glorious, pure, superior development of art, that one could do no better than to abandon all that had come before and devote oneself to the brilliant glow of antique art. Winckelmann was the inspired prophet of this new artistic position in Germany; his *Geschichte der Kunst des Altertums*, a book whose appearance precisely marks the boundary between the art of two epochs, was the key for all that followed.[16] The most recent period of art commences at this point. This second great artistic revolution gave birth to the art of the nineteenth century.

No name has yet been found for this artistic period; its multiform, disordered image, its zigzag movements, the great depressions throughout its development, make a characterization difficult. The Age of Idealism, the name advanced for the most important period, appears paradoxical[17] in view of the artistic conclusion to which this idealism has led us. Perhaps we would not completely err if for now we called it the age of artistic chaos.

Numerous factors worked hand in hand with the radical change that burst upon the artistic life of that period to produce this chaos. This condition was brought about, above all, by the wrong paths on which architecture and—quite necessarily in its train—the applied arts embarked. For the second time in the development of our Nordic art, all tradition was allowed to collapse. The architect ignored the playful grace of his previous art, that which he knew and practiced so incomparably well. Instead, he oriented himself to the ascending Greek ideal with its allegedly purer and more harmonic lines. The excellent training by which every artisan became skilled in the earlier forms was of no avail to him here. This highly developed art of the craftsman obviously could not be extinguished immediately but was left to die a slow death. It is most instructive to observe how this art declined from decade to decade and how the final remains of this perfected Rococo fell into the whirlpool of the nineteenth century. Who among us does not recall its final death sigh—the swirling sofa trimmings and the particularly degenerate swirl of the cornice ornament on the wardrobes of the 1860s and 1870s?

HELLENISM IN GERMANY: SCHINKEL

Architecture initially overcame this dilemma better than the crafts. It passionately embraced the forms of Greek antiquity and was, at least, able to realize works that evinced a high, outwardly formal perfection that could excite the enthusiasm of all the cultured people of that time. In every country of our Western culture, the ideal of the so-called pure antique began its mastery—most strongly in Germany and France.

Germany in that period had the good fortune to possess an architect whose genius raised him above the level of the rest of the world: he was Schinkel.[18] This genius would have achieved great things under whatever circumstances, but it is significant how even he was unconditionally controlled by the tendency of the time, which, so to speak, marked his particular sphere of activity. If other architects were more or less intimidated by classical forms, Schinkel's genius reached so far that he ruled and mastered even his more confining circle of Greek forms. Thus in his masterpieces—the Altes Museum, the Schauspielhaus, and the Neue Wache, all in Berlin—Schinkel created works that speak an eloquent language beyond the spirit of their time. In order fully to grasp the greatness of this man, however, we must examine the designs in which he achieved his best; we must, above all, peruse the Schinkel exhibit installed in the Technische Hochschule in Berlin, where the visitor will apprehend with astonishment his all-encompassing artistic spirit. He possessed an effortless facility in every branch of the plastic arts—painting, sculpture, crafts. He thoroughly mastered the figure, was excellent in landscape, unexcelled in conceptual design. He sat firmly in the artistic saddle; he was in a position to place the whole of the plastic arts in the service of his single great idea: Architecture. Schinkel is the last great, comprehensive genius that architecture has produced—the last grand architect, so to speak.

Through him the Berlin architecture school was thrust into the foreground. In other German cities the enthusiasm for Greece was no less warm. Through the aegis of art-loving King Ludwig I,[19] the city of Munich and Leo von Klenze entered upon a time of unfolding Greek architectural ideals that yielded the Glyptothek, the Propyläen, and in a wider sense, also the Pinakothek with its Renaissance forms.[20] Nothing is more characteristic than that this Greek enthusiasm made it fashionable to introduce these wholly uncommon Greek names over which the tongue of the German philistine had to stammer. The Walhalla in Regensburg and the Befreiungshalle in Kelheim are other fruits of this Munich school. In Vienna a Greek tidal wave began late with the buildings of Theophil von Hansen, which were themselves freely formed and already charged with the name Greek Renaissance.[21] In any case, the classicizing school of Berlin remained preeminent. Here Greek classicism held such a firm footing that an autonomous school with local coloration sprang from it; only here did its mastery spread over decades, certainly over the most significant part of the nineteenth century.

It was reserved for the specifically Berlin spirit, which always pursues criticism and intellectual activity, to develop a "scientific explanation" of the spirit of the ancient building-art.[22] Bötticher's *Tektonik der Hellenen*, a work conceived in the last years of Schinkel's life, appeared to all the world as a revelation in its elucidation of art and became a sensation in its time; up to a decade ago it was still referred to with the greatest respect.[23] But soon freer artistic views stirred again. In part, one began to look upon the art of the past from a broader perspective; in part, one again realized that art was not concerned with explanations but rather with effects,[24] which could not be further defined through reason. From this perspective, Bötticher's artful construction had to collapse.

After Schinkel's death his students Persius, Stüler, and Strack practiced in his manner, obviously without attaining the genius of the master.[25] Other major architects, like Hitzig, Lucae, and Gropius were more fortunate in that they entered upon freer paths of architectural design, even if remaining within the classicizing circle.[26] Among buildings of the latter sort, the Berlin Kunstgewerbemuseum by Gropius and Schmieden deserves special recognition.[27] It is a highly accomplished architectonic production displaying great originality.

NEOCLASSICISM
IN FRANCE

NEOCLASSICISM IN FRANCE

In France, a country that for centuries had the strongest and purest architectural tradition, Neoclassicism took an essentially different form than in Germany. Here the destiny of the State under the Corsican conqueror of nations created a fitting association with the Roman Empire, which influenced both architecture and the decorative arts. One felt Roman rather than Greek but no less enthusiastically. Instead of the pure Greek line, one paid homage to the decorative apparatus of the Roman Empire. The *style empire* then arose in France, characterized in particular by the work of the architects Percier and Fontaine.[28] From this movement at least one architectural monument of the highest rank was realized—Chalgrin's Arc de Triomphe de l'Etoile—a powerful work, full of tension and grandeur, whose architectural value, like that of the buildings of Schinkel, will survive the centuries.[29] A second work standing out from the mass of other buildings, the church of the Madeleine of Vignon, possesses none of the distinction of the triumphal arch despite its monumentality.[30]

As in Berlin, Neoclassical art was further cultivated in Paris. A classical school of architecture, more or less French in its character, developed within the rigorous courses of the Ecole des Beaux-Arts, which this highest Parisian academy has nurtured down to the present time. One highlight of the school, which soon incorporated and blended Renaissance and other components into a stylistic unity, is Garnier's great Opera.[31] Notwithstanding its heaving splendor and rather inflated architectural pretension, this is a work the consistency of which must arouse our admiration. We see an escalation of Garnier's architectural ostentation, perhaps to the point of being unbearable, in the Palace of Justice in Brussels by Poelaert—a work that one may perhaps mention in this connection, for it would be unthinkable without the Ecole des Beaux-Arts in Paris.[32] In any case, this architecture stemming from the Ecole des Beaux-Arts stands out in the nineteenth century for its exceptional assurance in detailing and high level of accomplishment. Its range of works is extensive and always of high competence. That this school could also produce works of the most noble simplicity, which thereby display today an almost modern character, is shown, for example, by the new additions to the Palace of Justice in Paris.

Neoclassical architecture played the most remarkable role in England. When Neoclassicism appeared, that spirit of strict Palladianism imported from Italy by Inigo Jones had dominated for more than a century.[33] Here a weighty and serious architectural direction, altogether unmoved by the Continental development of the Baroque and Rococo, had been able to celebrate unquestioned triumphs, even capturing the attention of the Continent. The monumentality of this architectural conception could not be intensified, and thus the introduction of Greek classicism did not have here the significance of a purifying or simplifying movement. It brought, on the contrary, a playful, almost soft element to the earlier gravity of architectural design, which can be seen most clearly in the buildings and interior decoration of the Adam brothers.[34] In addition, undercurrents of another, usually romantic, kind were already present, which denied unanimity to the nascent Greek enthusiasm. English architects, moreover, were generally able to project themselves into the Greek spirit only with a certain clumsiness. They did not seem to know what to do with the greatly admired antique architectural monuments and set them arbitrarily together, thus hitting upon the most remarkable conceits. The example known to all is the church of Saint Pancras in London. There the architect, H. W. Inwood, composed a tower in which he placed a copy of the Tower of the Winds in Athens upon the colonnade of the Erechtheum, and crowned both with the Monument of Lysicrates.[35] The architect Soane introduced no windows in the largest of the Neoclassical buildings, the Bank of England, because windows were not present in the art taken as precedent, that of the Greek temple (this reason, not security, was certainly the decisive one).[36] Thus he was forced to contrive all the lighting from interior courts. As a special ornament,[37] Soane placed on one corner of this windowless creation a copy of the round Temple of Tivoli.

NEOCLASSICISM IN ENGLAND

As laughable as such a puerile masquerade of architecture may appear to us today, the English were only passing into that absurd and dangerous tendency that attached itself to the architectural impulse of that time. If we today, now that the tidal wave of Greek enthusiasm has again receded, look back to the beginning of that period,

THE GREEK NARCOSIS

it appears to us as if these people had wandered in a dream. Wherever the architect set to work, an irresistible compulsion drove him to produce a copy of a Greek temple front. Whether it was a museum, a concert hall, a barracks, or a dwelling, or little guard house, the facade received Doric or Ionic columns with a temple pediment above. It made absolutely no difference what was behind the exterior walls; so long as the portico was built, the architect stood content and admiringly before his work, blind and deaf against every claim of reason.

Works of architecture, like a musical symphony or a decorative drawing, were understood solely as formal and abstract works of art for which the proposed practical problem served only as a pretext. Every constraint imposed on the requirements, however great, appeared permissible. Everything had to be subordinated to the delusion of a temple style that belonged to a time long past, to cultural conditions altogether dissimilar, to a climate completely different. What was not suited to the scheme—chimneys or roofs, for example—was suppressed, hidden, or masked. In this connection, Hansen's Vienna Parliament attained the peak of absurdity with its jutting central-heating chimney designed as an Ionic column, belching forth thick black smoke. Surely a satire on the derailed artistic views of a period could not be more caustically conceived.

Never in the history of art had there been such an infatuation. During the Renaissance, one had indeed pounced on the antique with similar enthusiasm, but there was a great difference between the two periods: then the model was essentially Roman, secular architecture; now, the Greek temple. The Renaissance masters limited themselves to Roman baths, palaces, circuses—that is, to those architectural ruins in which the translation of the old, rigid temple art to social needs was already accomplished. Now one was limited to the Greek temple, which had never had windows and whose rigidly constrained forms, the models of a so-called most pure and harmonious beauty, were as inflexible as they were believed to be inviolable. Indeed, the dominant artistic idea of the time was that the entire Renaissance had been unfortunately deceived about antiquity and that now, finally, the true, pure forms were in hand. How could one be allowed to dispose of these forms freely? The highest honor was to handle them "purely," that is, to copy them slavishly.

ITS
CONSEQUENCES:
POLITICAL
INFLUENCE

This rapture of enthusiam concealed the falsity that was then practiced under the name of architecture. It concealed still more. It concealed the rapid decline of craftsmanship noted above, indeed the gradual decline of architectural competence itself. Architecture had removed itself too far from reality, from a healthy contact with life, to be able to imbibe the daily nourishment necessary for its survival. Only the substratum of building production, the art of the master mason, remained healthy for a time. With it the old tradition endured, almost uninfluenced by the foolishness of high architecture, until the second half of the nineteenth century; it was overrun only when the architectural schools of a style-making academicism intervened and reached to the furthest corner of the land. **The decline of artistic trades was not only occasioned by the enthroned Greek temple art that neither could nor would make any use of the fine and graceful craft productions of the last blooming of the applied arts but also by political and economic factors.** [38]

The easygoing eighteenth century ended with a collapse of all social conditions. Above all, the Revolution entailed the fall of those privileged classes in whose hands the patronage of art had rested since Gothic times. The cavalier or nobleman, living according to his inclinations and experienced in courtly manners, was as if by vocation a connoisseur of art and a patron of the artist—this characteristic figure of three previous centuries disappeared from the scene.

More sober times arose and a new class came to the fore—that of the industrious burgher, the scholar, the civil servant, the businessman. If the nobleman had conducted his life in a more elevated manner, one in which devotion to the fine arts played a quite natural role and set an example for other social circles, if he embodied the spiritual and artistic refinement of his age, then the burgher took his place without this heritage, without the established duty to give the artist and the artisan commissions, without the need to cultivate a higher artistic culture.

At the outset, this new class also had more important things to do. The marauding expeditions of Napoleon occupied the entire world; the imperative task of the time, to stop this ingenious adventurer, taxed all energies to the limit. Finally, when peace again fell in the European house, the Germany that was not yet fully recovered from the wounds of the Thirty Years' War was exhausted to the point of prostration. Moreover, political tensions in the following decades further hindered the sense for a more engaged cultivation of art.

Thus art and the handicrafts quite naturally lost their footing, and a barbarism, such as our culture had not seen before, penetrated the substratum of the trades with little notice. The handicrafts absorbed the safe stock of traditional forms that, with the onset of the Greek artistic ideal, our second artistic revolution possessed in excess. Every initiative had its sources obstructed; the artist lived by plunder. Around the middle of the nineteenth century everything was finished; we no longer had any handicraft.

LOSS OF
TRADITION

THE NEW CLASS
WITHOUT
TASTE

The artistic condition now appeared grim in educated and middle-class circles. With the decline of the nobleman, not only was the protector of art, the connoisseur, and the patron lost but also the man of taste. The industrious burgher or scholar no longer possessed taste. A social characteristic of the nineteenth century can be seen in this absence of taste in educated circles. When the burghers with their newfound wealth turned their attention to art, they groped in the dark; they could not distinguish the noble from the base. Generally they were attracted, like the barbarian, to the gaudy and the vulgar. Attention to art often conveyed simply the wish to show off and to parade one's wealth. Thus arose another trait so characteristic for our time: the taste of the snob and the parvenu. A barbarism arose such as had not been known since late Roman times when the empire fell under the military emperors.

INDIGENT ART

Another contemporary indication of the distress of the nineteenth century was the so-called public patronage of art. Since there was no longer anyone who could sustain art, it was indigent and needed public support. Thus arose those orphanages and relief funds that we call museums, state art commissions, art associations, and the like—an artificial sustenance of the languishing artistic life through which much more was promised than could generally be attained. Indeed, the belief that museums could have conferred a truly appreciable and notable blessing on art must be counted as one of the disappointments of the last century; museums were nothing more than warehouses for art and the mere exhibition of art for the masses could not advance art at all.

THE STYLES OF
THE LOUIS

The distress was not so great in France as in Germany. Here the heyday of the first Empire period still nurtured the handicrafts, even if the refinement of the earlier decorative styles was no longer in vogue and a certain coarsening of feeling had occurred. Yet the steady demand for handicrafts soon returned the trade to the earlier French designs which, even modified over time, were on the whole strictly reproduced in the styles of the ancien régime. With this production France has continued to meet the entire European demand for high quality decorative goods and applied arts down to the present.

MIDDLE-CLASS
DOMESTIC ART

In this matter England has, like other cultured nations, for centuries fulfilled its aristocratic demands through France—and still does so. By comparison, the English middle class (and in the English social strata it outnumbers the aristocracy significantly) was completely independent; in the period when its architects were infatuated with Greece, it cultivated a unique and admirable bourgeois style of furniture, embodied by Chippendale, Hepplewhite, and Sheraton. With this, the ground was laid for genuinely middle-class household furnishings whose early development can also be observed somewhat later on the Continent in the so-called Biedermeier time—unfortunately soon to be trampled in the emerging battle of the styles.

Though not enduring the depressed economic conditions of Germany, the artistic life of England and France also grew ever more feeble with the passing decades of the nineteenth century. England reached its nadir around the middle of the century, a point even below that of Germany.

Since the beginning of the century (thus earlier than in other lands), there was in England another factor contributing to this problem. It would later make its effect tangible everywhere and be recognized as a further cause of the collapse of the crafts. It was the machine. The tremendous upheaval that this modern phenomenon wrought in every area of life first revealed itself in handicraft—cutting the ground from under it as indeed it still does today by more or less conspiring to its destruction. If the very existence of handicraft was thus placed in question, how little could one then worry about artistic qualities! It struggled for its bare existence.

THE MACHINE

While the handicrafts, the indispensable foundation of the entire artistic condition, were slowly hounded to death by hunger and persecution, our cultured class still enthused about what was presumed to be higher and purer in art, about the final harmonious unity of a world art for which it found the pretext in the notion of Greek classicism. This higher unity distinguished itself above all by hovering like a phantom in the air, never touching the ground of life. Appropriately, one called this the Age of Idealism. This so-called idealism found its most fertile soil in Germany, perhaps because the actual conditions here were the most dismal. Politically torn, economically poor, and by nature inclined to admire what is foreign, the Germans looked most longingly into the distance; thus that lamentable notion of artistic cosmopolitanism found here its most invigorating sustenance.

GERMANY AND
ITS IDEALISM:
THE ART
PROFESSOR

One saw in Greek art the eternal standard for the world, and thus forgot that there can be only one standard for art, namely that which expresses the life and culture of the time. One expended the greatest effort to grasp the so-called standard of Greek art in rules and formulas in order to employ it with ever greater confidence. Aesthetics, especially the development of artistic laws, shot up like a weed and occupied entire schools of philosophy. The aestheticizing professor of art, a new type of the nineteenth century, took up his post and informed, examined, criticized, and systematized art. He was all the more powerful the weaker was the pulse of art, the more withered the natural life of art had become. Thus the artist no longer ruled over[39] the arts of the nineteenth century, but rather the professor of art did. No longer did the artist speak artistically to the public, but rather the specialist on art did; and the world no longer sought to enjoy art but rather to be instructed about it. One was no longer touched by the work of art but rather criticized it. This state of affairs developed above all with and on the basis of Neoclassicism. The more idealistic one became, the more one distanced oneself from art; the more enthused one became about Greek art, the more impoverished was one's own soul.

This admiration for all things Greek, based on imitation, was like a narcosis into which the entire world, including our most eminent spirits, were drawn in the first half of the nineteenth century. Even a universal genius like Goethe stood under its influence, whereby he himself exemplified his own maxim that even "the greatest men are always bound to their century by a weakness."[40]

ROMANTICISM AND NORDIC ART

Just as every excess produces a countereffect, so also this Greek idealism evoked a reaction. This was the Romantic Movement. It discloses the second great artistic tendency of the nineteenth century. It too appeared in every country, admittedly in various degrees, and it is to be seen as the counterweight, as the revolt of the Nordic sensibility against the fundamentally contrary Greek classicism.

For the first time since the abandonment of the Gothic, we see again the sprouting of medieval artistic ideals, especially in the building-art. There was thus still an element in the Nordic breast that preserved the particular Nordic feeling for art; there still stirred the old inwardness of feeling that we encounter in medieval art at the expense of the outward sweep of the classical line. There was thus still present a remnant of that emotional warmth, inventiveness, and sense of workmanship, construction, and proficiency in the applied arts that strove to embody within itself that yearning for spiritualization, that desire for an intimacy suited to the circumstances or the individual task. In short, it was a striving toward the individual and the personal that had found such eloquent expression in the Gothic and in the whole of the medieval applied arts.

The Romantic Movement of the nineteenth century is of far greater influence than may appear at first glance; it was of immeasurable significance for all future artistic development. No stage in the development[41] of our culture is accidental; each one pursues its[42] purpose and accomplishes its necessary work. After the first flowering of a Gothic or Nordic art (so fundamentally different from the classical art of old), there had to be, as soon as the sources were opened, the imperative influence of an artistic culture that was still more powerful than the Gothic: the classical. The latter inundated the Germanic peoples almost completely for four centuries, no doubt carrying out a certain[43] educational work. But the tidal wave of the last phase of Neoclassicism carried its meaning to absurd lengths. It revealed the unsteady footing on which an art must stand in a time such as our own, so full of intellectual vitality; it openly revealed the contradictions with the spirit of the time and the national character. Now the genuine Nordic individuality could reemerge.

With this romanticism of the nineteenth century, the Germanic spirit once again claimed its rightful place. Today at the start of the twentieth century we can gauge its significance when we see not only the evident decline of all Latin peoples but also the decline of their cultural values and (what is here of particular interest) their art—when we see a newly created art, essentially produced by the Germanic peoples, cross over the threshold of the age.

The Romantic Movement, whose actual origin is to be found in an English poetry again inspired by nature, subsequently extended itself to all the arts, indeed to the entire spiritual life of the European peoples. Initially, it was a more or less obscure impulse; the Nordic peoples were hardly conscious of the full extent[44] of its significance. The first rendezvous of the early romantics, in fact, was Rome; the destination of romantic youth was Italy; the final refuge of many of its devotees was the Catholic Church. Nonetheless, the romantic compass of ideas was medieval and Nordic in its coloration, and its architecture, in particular, could only have its source in the Gothic building-art. In much the same way as with the newly discovered antiquity of the Renaissance, we now see the Gothic, whose works had been ignored for almost four centuries, everywhere newly discovered.

In Germany, the completion and restoration of the cathedral of Cologne captured the romantic attention for decades. This same romantic enthusiasm extended for the most part to all surviving medieval monuments.

With regard to the latter, we certainly can now look back on this activity only with mixed feelings. Although motivated by the best intentions, our blind zeal to alter our surviving medieval monuments must be termed barbaric from the perspective of later times. Just as earlier centuries completed and reworked newly discovered antique statues, almost fully destroying their value, we restored old churches, destroyed parts and added others, reworked whole buildings, and were at times so naive as to flatter ourselves that we could improve upon the old masters. In this manner,

THE
RESTORATION
RAGE

precisely those exemplars of art upon which enthusiasm was now fixed were often deformed and violated to the point of unrecognizability—such that they are as good as worthless[45] for all later times. In this, one thing was characteristic. Every architect who restored an old building believed that he understood the spirit of the ancient art completely, and thus only he was able to restore it faithfully in the manner of the ancients. Yet anyone who saw the restoration ten years later immediately recognized the artificiality and falseness of the work. This continues to the present day. Even now revivalists maintain that they can faithfully and truly restore the style and sensibility of the ancient art. And they are greatly irritated at the suggestion that in ten years their error will be apparent to everyone. The only conclusion to be drawn from past experience is that it is absolutely impossible to view things in the spirit of another time—this conclusion they nervously fail to draw. **Architectural preservation is still today,** especially in Germany, **in its infancy. So long as we do not see these** ancient buildings **as historical documents (whose infringement, even in their defective condition, is a historical offense), we can only hope that every old building—to its benefit—will for now escape the notice of restorers.**

NEOGOTHIC IN
GERMANY That we with all our admiration even dared to approach these medieval buildings in such a manner revealed how foreign their spirit had become to the present. We needed decades to reacquaint ourselves with them; we needed scrupulous research and an intensive love to approach that spirit again. Both were plentifully bestowed, and thus gradually there matured a school of architects skilled in medieval practices, which almost restored medieval art to full vigor. At the outset, the movement chiefly emanated from Munich, where in the first half of the century Friedrich von Gärtner built a series of monumental buildings in the Romanesque style.[46] It soon spread over central and western Germany, however, and made itself at home in cities like Hannover (where Hase worked), Cologne, and Kassel (under Ungewitter, whose admirable books contributed much to its diffusion).[47] In a few cities, such as Hannover, local Neogothic schools developed and imparted their particular character to the new architecture. Berlin, a classicistic stronghold, managed to resist the Gothic longer than elsewhere; in general, the medieval movement manifested itself only rather late in northern Germany, and then primarily in the revival of Nordic brick building, whose most significant representative was Johannes Otzen.[48]

NEW CHURCH
BUILDING The Neogothic was unable to win more general significance, despite a lifetime of work by a generation of enthusiasts in Germany. Apart from the local achievements

already mentioned, its use remained limited to churches, and even here the conservative nature of the efforts imposed a certain archaeological character, not only from a formal viewpoint but even with regard to the plan, which proved to be confining and against which every means was needed to battle it successfully. This battle was taken up by a younger group that, under the slogan "Protestant Church Building,"[49] demanded modern spatial configurations, more appropriate to the Protestant service than those handed down from the Middle Ages. Almost inevitably the plans of the northern Baroque were adopted, which embodied[50] Protestant thought to a significant extent. Today German church building is played out between these two parties. The former still remains by far the more powerful, although one may suppose that the future will increasingly declare itself for the latter.

In Vienna, the Gothic was favorably introduced by Heinrich von Ferstel's impressive Votivkirche.[51] The Gothic movement later found a significant exponent in Friedrich von Schmidt, who with genuine romantic enthusiasm preferred to call himself a Gothic stonemason, all the more so as he understood how to sustain somewhat more flexible views in the use of Gothic forms.[52] Best known is his Rathaus in Vienna, a large, disciplined work whose worth extends well[53] beyond the limits of the interest in styles.

The course of the Romantic Movement in French architecture was quite like that in Germany. Here, too, it was first concerned primarily with the restoration of old monuments. We also see it used in France predominantly in church building; here, too, indeed far more than in Germany, the Romantic Movement receded against the classical. Yet from the ranks of the French Neogothicists there ascended one figure who would have uncommon influence in advancing medieval architectural ideals throughout Europe: Viollet-le-Duc. He was the author of the immortal books *Dictionnaire de l'architecture* and *Entretiens sur l'architecture*—epoch-making volumes in which a boundless industry stored up treasures for generations, and from which there speaks a purity of constructional sensibility and an unqualified capacity for persuasion.[54] One would not hesitate to count these studies among the best of the century. As a practicing architect, Viollet-le-Duc was principally active in restoration, in which he obviously stood entirely under the yoke of his time and did far too much. Thus with the same hand that—to his honor—knew to guide the pen with such inspiration, he destroyed many faithful testimonies of earlier times.

Notably, the Gothic has played a much lesser role in recent French church building than have the earlier styles, especially the Romanesque and the Byzantine. Among the numerous new churches of this type, two mighty works, especially their

NEOGOTHIC IN
FRANCE:
VIOLLET-LE-DUC

interior spaces, stand out in their originality and acclaimed mastery of means: Vaudoyer's Marseilles cathedral and Abadie's Sacre-Coeur, still under construction on
Montmartre in Paris. [55] In the latter work in particular, we find evident the same high
ability and clear understanding of specifically architectural values that also distinguishes the new French school within the classicistic architectural movement.

TEST OF
STRENGTH OF
THE GOTHIC IN
ENGLAND

In England, the matter was pursued quite differently than on the Continent. Here
Gothic sensibility seemed naturally closer at hand, indeed there were even a few regions in which the old Gothic spirit survived from the Middle Ages. Here romantic
literature also appeared as a more compelling authority than on the Continent.
Above all, those literary masterpieces of Walter Scott powerfully prepared the way
for medieval artistic ideals. [56] Thus it happened that in England the development of
the romantic building-art preceded that of the Continent by about twenty years. And
not only this, it also occurred with much greater force; it was a thoroughly national
movement, against which—contrary to what happened on the Continent—the classicistic school declined in significance. This is expressed early on most clearly in the
great competition of the 1830s for the Houses of Parliament, which stipulated the
Gothic. The construction of this gigantic building by Barry, assisted by the highly
gifted architect Pugin (the actual founder of the Neogothic movement in England)
constituted the advanced school for a fully developed Neogothic practice of art, in
which England stood alone. [57]

Yet another factor assisted in this matter. A religious reform movement, com-
bined with a zealous reawakening of religious life, provided the building-art with
religious tasks in great numbers. An unprecedented sense of sacrifice by a bourgeoisie of long-standing wealth provided almost unlimited means for the construction
of churches. These times were most propitious for a brilliant period of Neogothic
building in England. The names of the architects Pugin, Scott, Street, and Pearson
shine as bright stars in the firmament of nineteenth-century English architectural history. [58] The works of the last-named master in particular express a command of the
means of a genuinely Nordic building-art, such as has not otherwise been achieved.

Yet certainly one was also deceived in one respect: in the notion of being able
to revive medieval art as a vital contemporary art. Precisely in England the greatest
efforts were made in this direction. Since the construction of the Houses of Parliament, England had gone to the greatest pains to establish a Gothic handicraft, to
reorganize the crafts in a Gothic manner. The entire architectural community was
occupied with the problem of adapting Gothic architecture to secular building. Even
if in both matters very good[59] results were achieved that after all merit our unqualified

admiration and indeed stand alone in the history of the Gothic revival, they would not be enduring achievements: no new Gothic tradition would develop. Even with the most vital organism in the field of architecture, the dwelling and its furnishing, results were sought that at best fall into the category of the curious. This Gothic furniture and those Gothic villas, on whose creation decades wearied themselves, today appear merely whimsical, indeed almost ludicrous. For the past twenty years in England the Gothic has been suppressed in public architecture, and even in church building it no longer prevails. The English example will dispel the illusion of anyone who still believes today that by a greater focus on the revival of medieval architecture we might find some salvation from the artistic chaos.

Nonetheless, with its more careful and extensive cultivation of the Romantic Movement in building-art, England gained something that amply made up for every expenditure and that every country can envy: first among all peoples it has developed a modern and at the same time wholly national art. In the 1860s there began to form that which we have learned to designate as the modern English style, and indeed the development occurred in direct connection with the Gothic. The father of this new artistic movement was William Morris;[60] its focal point was the furnishing of the English house; its thesis was sound workmanship, reasonableness, and sincerity; and its motive was a genuine, popular enthusiasm for art, which had been particularly kindled by the widely read books of Ruskin.[61] Everyone knows the triumphal march of this art about ten years ago to the Continent, where it powerfully stirred people's spirit and spurred them on to the same goals. This triumph would not have been possible without the profound English concern with the Gothic, without the spirit of the people saturating itself with the new artistic ideals derived from it.

THE NEW ART IN ENGLAND

The Gothic was unable to attain such an importance on the Continent, which was still haunted by the old Greek and Italian ideals of beauty. Still, the adoption of Gothic in schools as one of the main subjects in architectural instruction scattered many good seeds in Germany. In this connection, the highly gifted teacher Karl Schaefer in particular exercised a decisive influence on the younger generation.[62] A new, more sincere type of artistic sensibility was gradually cultivated, which as in England was the fertile ground for new departures in art. This was especially true for a vernacular conception of art and for ideals that could be described as Germanic-Nordic in contrast to the classical. However, as long as the outward form of the Gothic was and will be summarily taught as the value to be striven for, the spirit by

GOTHIC INSTRUCTION IN GERMANY

which alone it can succeed as an educational goal cannot yet unfold in full freedom. To this end, there must yet be a future struggle for a farsighted command of the field.

The classicistic movement that predominated[63] in Germany, notwithstanding the Gothic and romantic trends, underwent major changes before its position seriously[64] began to falter. As already noted, the strictly classical manner of a Schinkel was transformed by his followers into a freer practice, and thus the step from Roman models (as observed, for example, in Strack's Nationalgalerie in Berlin) to those of the Italian Renaissance was not very[65] exceptional. The Italian Renaissance thus soon became the universal watchword. Its principal representatives in Berlin were the collaborating architects Kyllmann and Heyden, and Ende and Böckmann; Ferstel and Hasenauer in Vienna; and Leins in Stuttgart.[66] Yet in Germany the brilliant Gottfried Semper, who after Schinkel was indeed the most important figure in the historicist movement in architecture, towered above them all. Among his numerous buildings, the Dresden Hoftheater is particularly distinguished for its great mastery of every creative means of architecture. He was, moreover, one of the most important writers on architecture of the century; his book, *Der Stil in den technischen und tektonischen Künsten*, has achieved world renown.[67] To be sure, whoever will take the pains today to immerse himself in the arguments of this book will immediately recognize how closely it is allied to certain prejudices of the time in which it came into being. This was the time of the most ardent battles over the styles—between the romantics and the classicists. Semper stood so much in the latter's camp that he could speak of the medieval building-art only in the most disdainful terms. The Gothic was to him "a rigid system," the classical antique movement was the "free personal." What a play with words! Furthermore, Semper also recognized and perceived no Nordic artistic conception; he perceived its every manifestation down to the present as only unwelcome deviations from his great world art—the antique. The whole tenor of Semper's work can be altogether understood as the outpouring of that cosmopolitan architecture that German Neoclassicism had created. A cosmopolitan architecture of the future, based on the antique, was its goal.

Whereas these efforts were oriented to the other side of the Alps, an event of a seemingly external nature, yet for Germany of universal significance—the Franco-Prussian War—brought a sudden change. It thrust the flame of patriotic fervor into the muddled artistic efforts of the time. As it did in every other respect, it also led to an artistic upheaval: it sparked the general revival of the German Renaissance. Next to the classicistic tidal wave that opened the century, the German Renaissance Movement was the most powerful event of German architecture and especially arts and crafts of the past century. Relative to the first, it had two great advantages: it was national and consequently more popular, but above all it had a profound influence on the crafts. Its inspiration for the applied arts was greater than its effect on architecture. Under its influence schools, associations, and museums of the arts and crafts were founded throughout Germany; the invaluable result was a resurgence in the vitality of the arts and crafts[68] and an expansion and deepening of new interests. Thus the basic condition for further expansion was provided. All that has since taken place in this regard derives from the movement initiated at that time, which in Germany assumed a similar, if also in the nature of things a less fortunate, role than the Gothic revival had played in England.

Great stylistic confusion obviously still reigned. Even here, architecture and the applied arts were content to glean—with eager hands—the rich harvest so readily supplied from the formal treasury of old art. Such a situation, however, necessarily yielded a certain dissatisfaction; a time had to come when one tired of the uniform, predigested fare and longed for a change. Thus it followed quite of itself that one quickly turned to later periods of art as soon as one became satiated with the earlier one. Like a hungry herd, architects and artisans[69] in the last two decades grazed over all periods of artistic development subsequent to the German Renaissance for their models. A stylistic battle began, in which the late Renaissance, Baroque, Rococo, Zopf, and Empire were slaughtered indifferently and, after a short period of blood sucking, were cast in the corner. What could then be more logical than that we would shortly find ourselves confronted by nothingness?

THE BATTLE
OF THE STYLES

This moment arrived only a few years ago. It is probable that history will close the chapter of nineteenth-century architecture with this event and deem the superficial repetition of all past styles as the essential characteristic of this period. During this period we saw the mighty tidal wave of Greek classicism spread out; running alongside it as its major competitor was the Romantic Movement, which nevertheless had but relatively little influence in Germany; and toward the end of the century we saw the reproduction and competition of every style of the last four hundred years. Symptomatic was the decline of all handicraft tradition and the impossibility of creating new, enduring connections to earlier periods—which both the Neogothic and the Renaissance movements had expected and attempted. Hand in hand with these

OUTCOME

events came a decline of the natural support of the arts and of public taste, which had already appeared at the turn of the previous century. These phenomena reached their low point in the middle of the nineteenth century, against which all efforts of the state and of public associations struggled without result. Thus the feature of the entire century is artistic decline and artistic muddle in every guise—the condition of artistic chaos the most striking image.

II

And yet it would be wrong to conclude the preceding survey of recent architectural development with an altogether negative result. The life of a time is so diverse that categorical generalizations always appear risky, and then too the large, most obvious events are not always the only essential ones. Even as these events come to fruition, seeds of a new beginning are cultivated beneath the surface, and usually a countermovement begins to form against the status quo. Furthermore, no wrong path in any course of development is so devoid of use and purpose that it does not bring at least some good with it. This applies to the architectural development in the last century as well.

If we observe, for example, what the best of contemporary architecture seeks, relative to the more unified and restricted art of previous centuries, we note that it employs a much more varied range of expression than any of the historical styles. Thus, with regard to the individual building types, today we seek to characterize their particular purpose through architectural design: for example, we seek to express the civic in a town hall; the majestic in a princely palace; the domestic and intimate in a villa. We seek architectural forms expressing the sublime in a monument to heroes, the somber in the mortuary chapel, the festive and joyous in the ballroom, the charming in the boudoir, and a sense of coziness in the tavern. Earlier periods of art generally had no such goals; they did not differentiate the means, whether they designed a church or a ballroom.

NEW GOALS IN ARCHITECTURE: GIVING CHARACTER TO ARCHITECTURAL WORKS

How have we arrived at such demands? Obviously it was through the schooling that we acquired[70] in coursing through the historical styles. There we saw the most varied aspects of mood set out in the different styles. We came to know, for example, the civic and the intimate in the building-art of the German Renaissance, the sublime and noble in the antique, the light and pleasing in the Rococo. What could be more natural than that we, in our lessons reciting the earlier forms of art, became accustomed to this diversity and range of expression, and that we, after our graduation from the course, wished to employ this knowledge at our pleasure. Thus there grew from the apparently senseless battle of styles in the nineteenth century a higher artistic demand in modern architecture: that of the unified command of all the means made available by earlier culture and their exploitation for a higher artistic purpose.

But it is well to remember that this is not a matter of treating this particular problem in a historically correct Gothic, that one in German Renaissance, and a third in the forms of Greek antiquity. We should have already disposed of this phase through the school of stylistic imitation. Since that approach is finished, it is now a matter of managing these means freely in the manner of the master who breaks the cast, for whom only the presentation of the idea is central and who sees all architectural forms as only the tool or outward means for his higher purpose. It follows that, stylistically speaking, architecture today stands on the threshold of a new time—indeed, a time that has increased its demands by leaps and bounds, and in which success requires a much greater artistic ability than that which has typically been required in the certain command of the individual styles.

NEW
CONDITIONS

Still other recent demands have imposed themselves on the building-art during the past century. Though unnoticed by most and pushed into the background by the prominence of the stylistic hustle and bustle, these new demands have nevertheless aroused a kind of undercurrent that promises to[71] be crucial for an emerging new architecture. These are the demands that result from new conditions of economics and transportation, new principles of construction, and new materials. With regard to the latter, the nineteenth century gave us two new building materials: iron and glass, which at the same time proved so useful in the extraordinary expansion of transportation and other new systems. These conditions yielded a few new building types of importance, above all the railway[72] terminal and exhibition building. With both types the fundamental requirement was a broad space with the maximum of light. In such cases iron and glass appeared the inevitable materials.

England showed the world the way in exhibition architecture with the construction of the Crystal Palace for the first world exhibition in 1851. For its time this was a unique undertaking, a marvel of the then still-blossoming English entrepreneurial spirit. The Crystal Palace was built by a gardener, the subsequently knighted Joseph Paxton, who was enlisted as a consultant because there was concern to preserve a row of trees within the exhibition building.[73] His experience with greenhouses brought him to this singular construction of iron and glass. In Paxton's time it was hardly considered architecture, and yet his prototype opened the way for a new architectonic phenomenon of the following decades: the wide-span iron-framed hall. This construction was particularly suited to a series of exhibition palaces for world expositions in France. Indeed France (where the brilliant architect Labrouste had still earlier given iron a prominent role in his Bibliothèque Sainte-Geneviève and Bibliothèque Nationale), as the nation of the great exhibitions, assumed the leadership in this field of construction.[74] The most splendid accomplishments of iron architecture were realized in the great Galerie des Machines and the Eiffel Tower of the exposition of 1889. These were works in comparison to which all the buildings of the last world's fair [Paris, 1900] represent an embarrassing regression. This step backward was, in any case, already anticipated in America. To the astonishment of a world expecting something quite new, the Americans, at [the Columbian Exposition of 1893 in] Chicago, knew nothing better than to hang the familiar antique masquerade costume on the iron ribs of its exhibition halls. However enchanting this fairy tale image may have been, this backward-looking production counted for less than nil in terms of artistic progress.

The constructional principle of the iron-and-glass exhibition palaces soon extended to other realms. The railway terminal, the market hall, the museum with a skylit central court, the broad glass-vaulted hall in every form, and finally also the urban commercial building with its extensive glass surfaces opening onto the street are all offspring of the same concept. The commercial building has developed particularly well in rapidly growing Berlin. It embodies a true cultural accomplishment of Berlin, attaining what may be termed a classic example in the Wertheim Department Store of Alfred Messel.[75] In this work, Messel almost unintentionally created something completely modern, especially in the way that he expressed new formal concepts in a logical and unbiased manner. Still more extensively than in the commercial buildings and department stores, iron and glass have been used in the public transportation stations, to which modern man's enormously intensifed drive for mobility has given such great emphasis. It would be quite wrong to want to exclude such buildings

EXHIBITION
BUILDINGS

IRON-AND-
GLASS
BUILDINGS

from strict artistic consideration, for they grow completely out of modern needs and are built with modern means. Certainly many aestheticians deny the artistic nature of iron construction, usually with the thesis that iron has too little corporeality to bring about monumental effects—a thesis that sounds very academic and merely imposes old perceptions onto the new. Had mankind found no other building material than iron, who would doubt but that we would also have created artworks with it? The only difference would be that we then would have had a different aesthetic perspective. But even the iron structures that already exist speak a language that is sufficiently eloquent to convince us artistically. **No one is able to resist the liberating and powerful impression made by the modern, wide-vaulted iron roofs**[76] **of our railway terminals,** even if for the time being they are not ordered artistically as historical styles. **These offspring of a new time and new aesthetic**[77] **belong to the realm of art as much as the church and the museum; indeed no one can object if**[78] **we view purely engineered structures, such as boldly arching iron bridges, as interesting expressions of human artistic creativity. In these works a completely new and modern cultural**[79] **spirit speaks, one which, as undeveloped as it may be, is born out of the most characteristic needs of our time and—far more than the efforts of architects that emanate all too much**[80] **from the imitation of styles—must be termed its genuine offspring.**

THE NEW
REICHSTAG
BUILDING

A building that for the first time united many of these new ideas and truly captured Germany's architectural interest was Paul Wallot's Reichstag building in Berlin.[81] The new ideas, not the least of which was his daring use of glass and iron for the exterior design of the cupola, were in fact the basis for much of the criticism of the building. It is a well-known phenomenon that artistic innovations will at first be rejected by most people—a circumstance that arises because popular judgments in art are almost exclusively derived from habit. The innovations of the Reichstag correspond in part with the previously noted demand for harvesting the fruit of all past styles: free artistic creation through the command of all preceding cultural production. From this mastery there resulted in this instance an individual, personal language of the artist in which indeed the forms of the past were unhesitatingly employed, but by working freely with the different stylistic qualities and creating unique, thoughtful values with them rather than simply reproducing one style. With such values, the enlistment of a specific style, as had become customary in the course of the nineteenth century, is denied. These values have their essence in the content, mood, and characterization of the particular. Thus every visitor to the Reichstag will be captivated by the somber, almost gloomy gravity of the south entry hall in which the whole space and ornamentation pursue the goal of transporting the visitor into a consecrated mood that anticipates the grandeur and significance of this monument. Every visitor will have experienced the effect of the great lobby in which the majesty of the imperial concept is movingly revealed. The innovative qualities clearly expressed for the first time in the Reichstag make it a building of creative distinction. With it, a new era in the German building-art begins; it is the transitional link to its future development. Indeed, Wallot is the only figure[82] in German architecture who created a school in the second half of the nineteenth century. Wallot introduced that sense for the massive monumental that the best architects of our younger and middle generation emulate—that grandeur that when free from the pursuit of style stresses the characteristic and encourages artistic emotion. This is the enormous service that Wallot has realized for German architecture. He himself forcefully expressed his view that the styles should be only a springboard from which the architect soars to his own independent creativity.

It must not be forgotten, however, that the architectural trend created by Wallot in this exclusively monumental sense harbors within it a certain one-sidedness. In the enormous realm that the building-art must serve in our social life—the solution of simple everyday problems—Wallot's program offered nothing. And one certainly cannot wish that it should extend its particular influence to this field, since the fantastic wealth of forms and the resulting high drama (even the Reichstag Building somewhat groans under a surfeit of forms) would be ruinous. Furthermore, extending this tendency would only intensify what is already a dubious trend in our contemporary everyday architecture: the exuberant growth of the purely formal.

One error[83] of the architecture of the last century was indeed that it sought to make[84] monuments from everyday tasks. In virtually every earlier time, at least in those in which the practice of art still retained an indigenous quality, a distinction between a monumental building-art and a simple middle-class building-art was observed.[85] In addition to the architecture based on the precedent of historical monuments, there had always existed a building practice based in the arts and crafts that emanated from the guild, which satisfied one's everyday needs in dwellings and in other ordinary artifacts.[86] In this production one disregarded the use of higher artistic means. One remained simple and natural, limited oneself to the necessary and familiar, and generally followed a timeless local guild tradition on which the changes in monumental architecture had only a limited[87] effect, if any at all. This tradition stood fast on the ground of practical needs, on local conditions, and above all, on common sense.

This type of building practice generally[88] disappeared during the nineteenth century. Like handicraft, it received its deathblow with the advent of the Greek enthusiasm and after that, in the sickly condition in which it suffered for a time, was completely overrun in the chase after the historical styles. It barely survived into the second half of the nineteenth century.[89] Currently, it can be considered fully extinguished. Whoever visits our rural towns today will generally find in the newly realized "Bahnhofstrasse" that which has taken its place: those inauthentic, small-town buildings, reduced from the higher building-art, claiming to be "architecture" by the most labored means and for which our present schools of building technology are principally responsible. Only in the old town do we ordinarily still encounter the unfalsified guild tradition in older buildings that in their simple demeanor, effect a reinvigoration precisely through their opposition to modern buildings.[90]

These new streets leading to the railway stations of rural towns vividly reveal the bankruptcy that we have reached in the building practice related to our everyday tasks. We could also declare the "rental barracks" of our great cities, overladen with stucco and imitating the palaces of princes, as unhealthy witnesses to our unhealthy urban condition. But the countryside demonstrates that today the poison has reached everywhere,[91] that our everyday building practice is polluted even at its lowest levels—by the exertions of an irrelevant architecture-mongering, by the formalism and academicism that the artistic wanderings of the nineteenth century draped over that practice.

Every borrowing of old or[92] foreign precedents in architecture harbors the danger of inducing formalistic misdirections. It is the curse of every derivative style that we see and admire in the model only the form, whereas in any genuine art the form is only an expression of the inner nature, a result of contemporary developments. Our historical knowledge, so unexpectedly enlarged in the last century, which was also extended to the historical building-art, should at least discourage us from direct borrowings. For this knowledge reveals to us the totally different conditions on which the existence of our old buildings was based and on what a totally different conceptual basis they were built, what wholly different purposes they served.[93] What we admire in those old buildings today is in no small part values that we, for whatever sentimental reasons, have artificially drawn from[94] them—partially have fantasized into them. Consider that the now so much admired painterliness of old buildings was rarely originally intended but rather almost always arose naturally from existing requirements, in part developed through additions and reconstructions. Such values, as well as the particular designs[95] that we encounter in old cultural objects, can be grafted onto a new work only with a loss of their artistic authenticity. For artistic authenticity resides in the full correspondence of essence and form, not when the nature of the thing is sacrificed to an imported form.

The formalism of the nineteenth century, nurtured by a purely cultural classicism that unconditionally set the tone of this era, extended itself also to the romantic building movement, even though the latter actually should have protested the chains that formalism had laid on mankind through classicism.[96] In the same manner, our Gothic revivalists became entangled in the creepers of external forms and, like the classicists, degenerated into mere architecture-mongering. That they found sure refuge in church building was only because nineteenth-century church life itself had more or less sunk to a shadow existence, one that lacked the cultural authority of earlier religious times. If the Christianity of the future, with greater decisiveness than it has shown up to now, should see its task in the actuation of Christian deeds (perhaps even in the solution of the social question, rather than beingcontent with the hymns and prayers of the parishioners), then new architectural tasks might arise from such a modern change of program—tasks that might no longer so unquestioningly be solved with Gothic claptrap. English and American religious buildings provide valuable pointers here in that they seek less the ideal of an emotionally appealing church space than that of a community house, in which are played out the richly developed, communally beneficial work and cultivation of Christian brotherhood.

Architectural formalism appeared most distinctly in the stylistic hunt that began with the German Renaissance of the 1870s and cursorily rushed through all the styles of the last four hundred years. This was nothing other than a jingling of forms in which a disastrous error was taken for "architecture." And not only did we feast on this inventory of forms for such elaborate architectural works as monuments, but we also, as noted above, imposed these images over the most harmless daily functions. Moreover, we were first misled in that we were attracted only to monuments of earlier times, whereas everyday buildings, which certainly could have offered sounder pointers, remained—to the extent that they have survived at all—[97] unobserved because of their modest appearance. Thus the forms of German Renaissance castles were transposed onto the small burgher's house. Thus we fell into the error begun in classicism of transposing the temple front or, as in the time of the imitation of the Italian Renaissance reproducing, at the slightest opportunity, the Palazzo Pitti at a diminutive scale.

How superficial the architectural hustle and bustle of the nineteenth century was in this respect is clearly demonstrated by the importance that the word style assumed. Previously there were no styles, but rather only a straightforwardly prevailing artistic direction to which everything was subordinated as self-evident truth. In the nineteenth century, mankind was for the first time expelled from this artistic paradise, having plucked from the tree of historical knowledge. For decades architects feuded among themselves over the worth of the various styles; classicists and romantics confronted one another as warring parties[98] and expended their best efforts in attempting to prove the superiority of one style over another. Even today the very slight interest that the public brings to architecture collapses into the concept of "style." The layman's first question about a new architectural work concerns its "style." One is proud to be able to recognize the styles, and the capacity to differentiate the various styles suffices even for those who wish to be considered knowledgable about architectural matters. The world lies under the spell of the phantom "style-architecture." It is hardly[99] possible for people today to grasp that the true values in the building-art are totally independent of the question of style, indeed that a proper approach to a work of architecture has absolutely nothing to do with "style."

As in the last century we became accustomed to regard architecture solely from the viewpoint of style, so there was the demand for the discovery—alongside the historical styles—of a new style, the style of the present, which could also only be sought in purely outward appearances. In fact, attempts were not lacking to arrange the outer stylistic dress of buildings in a manner that at the time looked modern. One need only recall the Maximilianstrasse laid out in Munich under Maximilian II,[100] those buildings in which the development of the new style was sought by blending antique and Gothic details—an undertaking that appears to us today in all its miserable failure as childish. To such attempts must also be added the most recent efforts to seek the essence of a modern style by pasting modern plant ornaments and sapling motifs onto the old organism: that is, surrounding column capitals with naturalistic plant forms rather than with Ionic volutes or Corinthian leaves and giving the window surrounds wavelike forms rather than rectangular outlines. This type of modern style is, in almost all cases, only a debased edition of the earlier superficially employed historical styles, which it was supposed to displace. It absolutely remains in the realm of architecture-mongering imprisoned in a formal prejudice of which we rightly should have had enough.

For the new cannot arise in such outward appearances; architecture, like every other expression, presumes a vital presence. We expect new ideas, not commonplaces clothed in new words. Architecture, like all other artworks, must seek its essence in content to which the external appearance must adapt. We must also insist that its external form serve only to mirror this inner essence, whereby the kind of formal detailing, "the architectural style," plays a minor role—if it is not wholly insignificant.

From this point of view, a great part of contemporary architectural production fails completely, for its creators remain imprisoned in their efforts at a style. If we wish to seek a new style—the style of our time—its characteristic features are to be found much more in those modern creations that truly[101] serve our newly established needs and that have absolutely no relation to the old formalities of architecture: **in our railway terminals and exhibition buildings, in very large meeting halls, and further, in the general tectonic realm,**[102] **in our large bridges, steamships, railway cars, bicycles, and the like.**[103] It is precisely here that we see embodied truly modern ideas and new principles of design that demand our attention. Here we notice a rigorous, one might say scientific objectivity [*Sachlichkeit*], an abstention from all superficial forms of decoration, a design strictly following[104] the purpose that the work should serve. All things considered, who would deny the pleasing impression of the broad sweep of an iron bridge? Who is not pleased by today's elegant landau, trim warship, or light bicycle? Since such works stand before us as the products of our time, we see[105] a modern sensitivity recorded in them. They must embody an expressive modern form; they must mirror the sensibility of our time, just as the richly[106] acanthus-laden cannon barrel did the seventeenth century or the carved and gilded sedan chair the eighteenth century.[107]

In such new creations we find the signs indicating our aesthetic progress. This can henceforth **be sought only in the tendency toward the strict matter-of-fact [*Sachlichen*], in the elimination of every merely applied decorative form, and in shaping each form according to demands set by purpose.** Other signs, such as our clothing, confirm this. Men's clothing in the second half of the eighteenth century (at least for the nobleman)[108] retained the richest forms, bearing embroidered decorations that were made from costly, easily damaged materials. In the nineteenth century there was continuous simplification, leading up to today's unornamented dress and topcoat. Today's clothing is the same for all the classes of society: its singular characteristic is that it defines in every respect the middle-class ideal, whereas in the eighteenth century the particular customs, way of life, and clothing of the highest class set the standard. Even the king appears today, when not in uniform, as a simple burgher; there truly is no other form of clothing available to him—he is obliged to dress the same as his chancery clerk. Only in the military uniform has a remnant of the old, embellishing culture been retained; one can observe, however, that its days are also numbered now that the image of the lusterless and colorless military dress of the future, abstracted from soldiers' uniforms, appears on the horizon. Even with women's dress, which still takes artistic considerations into account to the highest degree, there are already transformations toward simplicity and unconditional functionality—changes which, stemming primarily from England, we express by the concept "tailor-made."

Nevertheless it would be dangerous to assume that merely satisfying purpose is itself sufficient. "Reform clothing," in whatever form it is recommended, affects us emotionally like a caricature. Today's simple clothing is also not without its unnecessary elements.[109] Our elegantly dressed gentleman still wears a top hat, patent leather shoes, and silk lapels—elements that might almost be compared with certain polished and nickel-plated parts of a machine. In both cases they seem to have been brought into being by a specific requirement for cleanliness—a demand not only to hinder undesired accumulation of dirt but also[110] to demonstrate symbolically that it is not present, that everything is neat and in the best of order. Our starched white linens also follow the same example.[111]

Thus there is a coincidence here of certain sanitary and aesthetic concerns. And the combination of the two appears everywhere[112] in modern designs as we now begin to see, for example, in our dwellings. Here, reforms are taking place—we recognize them most fully in the contemporary English house—that strive to increase the amount of light and air, to design strictly functional rooms, to avoid all useless appendages in the decoration, to eliminate heavy, unmovable[113] household furnishings, and to strive for an overall sense of brightness and impression of cleanliness. These reforms follow the same tendency as our clothing, the closer dwelling that envelops us.

In summary, our contemporary aesthetic-tectonic orientation may perhaps be seen in the fact that instead of developing purely external ornament that stands in no immediate relation to the essence of the thing, we now strive decisively toward functional design. Yet we also seek to present this form—more symbolically than practically—with a handsome elegance and a certain clean conciseness of form.

THE
PONDEROUSNESS
OF ARCHITECTURE

In the realm that we generally recognize as architecture, we do not find this distinctly modern tendency evident or in any way anticipated today. In considering architecture, we must first retain the already discussed distinction between works of the higher building-art and those of everyday tasks (monumental building-art and middle-class building-art), even if it must be admitted that this distinction must be taken quite generally and that no sharp boundaries can be drawn. An autonomous form is synonymous with the first category:[114] its division into a strong architectonic skeleton, the dominance of a strict rhythm here is as unavoidable as the regulated structure of a drama or the poetic form of a verse. With a monumental building we neither can nor should desire a realistic design that is strictly fitted to need.[115] The matter is, of course, quite different with the quotidian tasks, especially with the dwelling, where we clearly should disallow the demand to realize a higher artwork in a closed form. Such goals are as much out of place here, for example, as the journalist's intention to write a newspaper article in an epic form.

We must also consider that architecture is in its very essence a conservative art and perhaps cannot leave its accustomed tracks as easily as painting or the applied arts. For a building is always of considerably greater economic importance; its practical realization requires thorough preparation and depends on a multitude of external conditions with which the other arts need not concern themselves. Of all the arts, the building-art is the most ponderous.

Yet our previous architecture nonetheless turned its back on the efforts that everywhere find general validity, especially in the smaller tasks of daily life. Thus today architecture is not free from the appearance of a certain ossification and alienation from life. The superficial style movements that held all recent development spellbound are chiefly responsible for this.[116] A stripping away of such mere architecture- and style-mongering, which today controls almost the entire field, is necessary if we are to have a rejuvenation. Wherever possible we should for now ban completely the notion of style. When the master builder clearly refrains from any style and emphasizes that which is required of him by the particular type of problem, we will be on the correct path to a contemporary art, to a truly new style no longer so distant. When the master builder takes into account only the fact that one, above all else, sells in a department store, above all else, lives in a dwelling, exhibits in a museum, teaches in a school; when he seeks only to do justice, and indeed in every detail, to those demands presented by the site, the construction, the design of the rooms, by the ordering of the windows, doors, heating and lighting sources—then we would already be on the way to that strict straightforwardness [*strengen Sachlichkeit*] that we have come to recognize as the basic feature of modern sensibility. No one would maintain that all of these demands, whose justification is indeed properly at hand, are pres-

STYLE-
MONGERING

ently handled in a satisfactory manner. Today the average architect still works primarily in a stylistic way;[117] he builds either in a style derived from antiquity or in a medieval vein and, in fact, whenever possible with a high degree of exactitude with regard to the decade and region of the original style. If he builds in an antique or Italian style,[118] he forces the architectural body into the chains of rigid academic axes, suppressing every irregularity stipulated[119] by the conditions in favor of his formalistic scheme. Thus he lays out the windows, which appear throughout as identically framed holes in the wall, according to his imaginary axes rather than where they would be desired if considered by need or orientation; and he suppresses the roof, the chimney, and everything else that runs counter to his formalistic[120] view of a correct Italian facade. If he builds in a medieval or German Renaissance style, the magic word is "painterly." He then takes care to achieve purely superficial, often arbitrary groupings, which again have absolutely nothing to do with the essence of the thing. He introduces little towers, little gables, and oriels where they appear to him to be desired for the painterly grouping, and he lays out the stairs, if possible, in such a way that their ascending windows make a good image from the street. In both cases, he makes primarily a style-architecture,[121] rather than primarily solving the task in a straightforward [sachlich] manner. He creates a hallucination of abstract beauty under which the user can twist and turn as he will. The architect believes he is able to demand this sacrifice for the sake of his efforts at style and architecture. Indeed, he considers such style- and architecture-making to be his particular calling; his apparatus of columns, gables, roofs, and tower solutions are his special tools in the management of which he was trained in a building school according to the statutes of a guild, and from which he is of no mind to be separated. He busies himself above all else as a "style-architect."

THE ARTS AND CRAFTS MOVEMENT

With architecture's partiality toward a style and its inherently limiting ponderousness, it follows that it was not from architecture but from the arts and crafts, and not from architects but from artists of a quite different type, particularly painters, that the leadership came for that fundamental shift in our artistic situation that has been under way for a few[122] years under the designation of "the new movement." Only in Vienna, where the architecture school of Otto Wagner has already for some years worked toward an architecture that is both artistically freer and more considerate of the demands of purpose, was the building-art both able and inclined from the beginning to form an alliance with the newly arising crafts. In other places, particularly in Germany, the community of architects have till now acted quite negatively. Yet since the arts and crafts in the final analysis are only directed to the design of interiors, they work hand in hand with architecture, even if one understands architecture, as is customary today, under the narrow notion of erecting buildings. Success in the[123] new trend of the arts and crafts, therefore, cannot remain without influence on architecture; indeed this situation can lead to the result that the arts and crafts pull architecture along after them, just as the German Renaissance Movement of the 1870s also found its origin in the arts and crafts.

Even this narrower Arts and Crafts Movement itself obviously cannot be seen with absolute clarity. The movement in Germany presents itself still today as a bubbling brew of often antagonistic ingredients, which is far from presenting a united image.[124] This German movement, in the final analysis, is a descendant of the movement that arose under the leadership of William Morris in England in the 1860s, and yet it is nevertheless fundamentally different. Superficially, what most distinguishes the new Continental art from the English movement up to now is the luxuriant extravagance of form and the rage for sensational designs.[125] In Germany, the whole movement arose from the effort to seek[126] so-called new forms—that is, forms that basically should have nothing in common with traditional forms. If one now acknowledges this yearning, this discontent stored up for years in reeling off the old styles, to be the immediate cause for change, one should not forget that this change expresses a conception that, in essence, does not reach down to the true artistic questions of the time. Once again it is simply a matter of forms, thus once again basically the old miseries of style and ornament. What good does it do us if the old acanthus tendril is replaced by a linear squiggle? Does anyone really believe that such a superficial change will bring the artistic solution that we so much desire today?

In the meantime, someone who observes the matter more deeply, someone who does not allow himself to be misled by the violent way in which such superficialities are stretched here and there, such a person[127] will discover in the contemporary movement a more profound basis. And perhaps he will then come to expect[128] that this position concerning form—that which is still so generally[129] prevalent in the so-called new art of today—represents only a transitional stage; it is only in a teething period through which an ascending, truly new conception of art is about to unfold.[130]

    Compared with the earlier artistic practice that took place under the spell of historical styles, the new movement, when we consider the best achievements of its leaders, is better in many respects.[131] Instead of the merely pedantic forms[132] of earlier times, we now have a free and unfettered shaping of form,[133] which takes account of every special circumstance, which fluently adapts to every need, tacks down the inner essence of the problem, and seeks to express everything outwardly. Instead of a pedantic, academic approach to design, we have individualized it, and herein is already expressed a victory of the contemporary spirit that the movement embodies. From the beginning, it saw with great clarity its goal in the interior and comprehended it again for the first time since the days of old closed artistic tradition as a unified whole. [134] In addition to its more realistic elements, we also discern emotional elements. We strive for a certain emotional unity of color and form in the design of interiors, in which is exercised that refined sensibility to color that has been transplanted from the new rebirth of color in painting. In the shaping of form there is a preference for the soft, flowing line, which in its capacity for expressiveness, in any case, cannot be equaled by the stiff, straight forms that previously dominated. Only this new line, so it is said, can accommodate the finer gradations of the modern, strictly differentiated life of feelings, and capture the fleeting moods that modern man wishes to see embodied in a work of art. Thus this new Continental art up till now presents itself chiefly as an emotional art, revealing both its strengths and weaknesses. As an emotional art, it may provide support for and perhaps altogether capture our present emotional life. But it must remain conscious that it then moves onto the shifting ground of ever-changing values. Within the pendular sweeps of emotional values, the gravitational axis that alone within change is enduring and mathematically comprehensible will, for the tectonic arts, always be those necessary and constant demands of material, purpose, and construction. The more perfectly these are fulfilled, the more lasting will be the value that has been achieved. From the standpoint of these demands, however, the accomplishments of the Modern Movement thus far are not wholly successful.

Observe the errors that our lesser industrial artists have fallen into by falsely imitating the superficial traits of leading artists, errors that in the so-called Jugendstil or Secessionstil (the names with which manufacturers designate their latest fashions) appear worse than any of the earlier fashions that were cultivated under the banner of the historical styles. Even the art of the leading artists is often filled with contradictions. The already mentioned emotional whipping of lines, which originated in Belgium, does not take into account the material; it forces the ornament of the book, the brass candlestick, and the piece of furniture indiscriminately under its spell. With furniture design in particular, it demands irresponsible sacrifices in the treatment of construction and material, since the most evident property of wood is the clear directionality of its fibers. And even if today's technology can overcome any difficulty of construction resulting from this approach, and even if we have imported species of woods from overseas that are the most resistant to splitting, the entire joiner's trade nevertheless works in certain artificial relations. Above all, such practice is extremely expensive and its products remain beyond the broader spectrum of people. Taken very generally, treating a material in a way contrary to its nature is hardly in accord with the spirit of a time such as ours, which is characterized by very practical [*sachlich*] and sober thought. The new movement would gain much conviction and popularity if it displayed more naturalness and a healthy sense of workmanship. A strong dose of realism would do it enormous good. Then, too, its products would be available to the greater number of the people and its impact would be much greater. Today, no movement that seeks to be a reform movement can direct itself only to the production of luxury art; its goal, rather, must be to pursue an art suited to middle-class society, which defines the general character of our modern social condition.

But here we hit upon another new grievance of our contemporary state of affairs in Germany: our modern society does not yet have the desire to change its surroundings and see them artistically designed. It is in no position to do this, above all, so long as our present living conditions persist. In contrast to England where the much older movement had the opportunity almost from the beginning to see its natural base as the house, where through all levels of the society the desire flourished to live in one's own house and make it a permanent residence—the German has no proper house. Unsettled in a manner that appears to have retained something from nomadic life, he seeks his lodging in apartment buildings of factorylike production. The slight interest that he attaches to the rooms into which accident has thrust him, and which he changes as lightheartedly as a hotel room, is the cause of the cancer that afflicts the entire state of our German art.

In fact, a change in our German artistic situation can only take its start in the German house, which essentially is yet to be created. Art begins, like so much else, at home. Only he who takes an artistic interest in his four walls, who is naturally inclined to shape his personal surroundings artistically, will bring that sensitivity for art from his rooms into the street and the larger environment. And this is imperative if our contemporary world is again to have a broader, popular art.

And here the new movement created something completely novel, something that in its form as well as its character was fundamentally different from historical works. The historical interior, unless it was purely vernacular [*bürgerlich*], that is, wholly undecorated, could only be achieved with a surfeit of architectural forms and clichés. The Renaissance, including all its variants down to the present time, transferred the elements of exterior architecture—columns, pilasters, entablatures—to the interior, thus working with an

THE NEW
INTERIOR[135]

apparatus of forms that was intrinsically foreign to the nature of the thing. The new art developed the character of the interior from its own requirements. Above all, color became preeminent, for we are aware that it, more than architectural form, acts strongly and directly and creates an ambiance.

The interior of the new German Renaissance, that is, of the last thirty years, had atmosphere owing to the historical associations it evoked; it was the product of a backward-looking generation. The ambiance of the modern interior is more firmly grounded. Form and color are developed in unison and come to embrace one another in that they both strive to embody the same emotional constituents of feeling. It is not as if color and unity had played a trifling role in the old art—one need only think of Italian decorations and the interiors of the French Louis. But the feeling for color appears today refined and heightened; above all, broader perspectives of order prevail that employ a unified color scheme with the strictest consistency—so consistent that even the oriental carpet becomes alien. A ground color or basic triad always fixes the direction to which all else is then subordinate. In this, the basic conception of Whistler,[136] so undervalued in his own time, appears to find its first broader consequence—certainly the origin of the new emphasis on color in the interior is to be sought in the more recent development of painting.

THE WHIPLASH LINE   In the Modern Movement the definition of form is not quite so resolved as the consensus on color. To be sure, one also works here toward an expressiveness, particularly in that one seeks to clarify certain static images more forcibly than before with the vigorous assistance of human "empathy." The chair becomes something straddle-legged and crouching, the table leg an elastic line like the weight-bearing human foot. The constructive parts clasp one another; a metal attachment claws into the wood and extends itself like an arm; a brass handle indicates through its lines the motion with which it should be used. Or one may try to increase the utility of furniture through the rigorous adaptation of form to the physical movements of the human being. In both endeavors, one generally succeeds better with the curved line than with the straight one, so much so that the whipping of the line has actually become a dogmatic feature of the Continental Modern Movement. But the reasons for this whiplash have obviously more or less been forgotten; perhaps they have been avowed only in the program of a few creators and appear even there only by a labored abstraction from the unconscious will-to-form. We would not be amiss to assume that the whiplash curve was basically of a purely formalistic nature, an observation that is also supported by the fact that this line has been as prevalent in ornament as in structure. However that may be, we have today a style of the whiplash form with many German adherents in the arts and crafts, notwithstanding that it arose with van de Velde and arrived through him from Belgium.[137]

Yet what is still more significant is that fashion seized the whiplash line as the characteristic of the new style that it had so long awaited. Thereupon industry acted immediately to commercialize this new style. The principle of the whiplash line appeared so easy and simple; at last one had something tangible to utilize, something with which to manufacture. In no time the world had the Jugendstil.

THE JUGENDSTIL

It appears that the masses are incapable of grasping the fundamental nature of human problems. Somewhere an idea is born that contains an entire program for the future, that is capable of deeply influencing and advancing culture. The multitude, if it notices it at all, laughs it away. Then there steps forward a single form, a formula, a superficiality. Immediately this is taken as essential, puffed up, cried out, and taken as the heart of the matter. The spirit is driven out and the letter deified. Thus it has generally been in religion and morals; in a lesser way the same has come to pass again, as the whiplash curve was taken for the new art and the Jugendstil was founded upon it. Under its dominance people of fashion rejoice, the philistine frets, and the friend of art sighs. For a moment the world opened itself to a welcome liberation; the style-machine of the last twenty years had been driven to the absurd and the clockwork of stylistic imitation stood still. But this was true for only a moment. Immediately this opportunity closed upon itself as the whiplash curve and the little flower ornament emerged and worked with redoubled energy. Again there was a style, and now one that was indubitably the very latest.

Perhaps it is just as well that the formalism of this whiplash line (for it had degenerated to such even in the hand of its inventor) was put into the mill of industrial fabrication in order to play a role in the fashion market. Thus the warning was given that it would soon be brought to ruin. The more thoughtful were obliged to maintain their distance and thus perhaps to inch closer to the central question of the time. It is obvious that, compared to the German Renaissance and Rococo (the last styles that fabricators had in their clutch), the Jugendstil is no improvement. Previously one had the guideline of the treasury of forms of the old art, an art that had developed naturally. Whatever one produced had a certain character, even if a purely archaeological one. But now we sank into boundless caprice, deriving everything from the works of a few artistic personalities. From such a personal art we derived less understanding than from the historical styles. The new ornament that was to develop through a study of plants (which had been extolled as a solution) remained, in the hands of lesser artists, just as poor, insipid, and helpless as the art of the leader, when reduced by generalization to a watery soup. Thus with the so-called Jugendstil we have been led into a worse channel than that in which we sailed in the time of stylistic imitation.

The Jugendstil fashion demonstrates what an artist's art can become when it is broadcast to the multitude. In the realm of the applied arts, it demonstrates at the same time how little the greater part of the public is served by a strongly personal artist's art—at least directly served. A longer time is required for the particular qualities of an artistic personality to be fused in a tradition. The fusion will seemingly first be achieved by the next generation, by those who stand on the threshold of their lifeworks. We await from this generation both a generalization and a clarification of the numerous currently conflicting personal tendencies: we hope that this generation will shape a broader stratum with a more unified will and that it will do away with the Jugendstil, which only proved that incompetents had picked the fruit of the new movement too early from the tree. The Jugendstil was invented by those still pandering to the sensibility of a parvenu society that desired pretentious and heavily decorated ornamental art—and for whom the understanding of the true modernity, which lies in an appropriate straightforwardness [*Sachlichkeit*] rather than in applied ornament, had not yet dawned.

THE ORNAMENT CRAZE

Obviously this principle has not yet been clearly recognized by our leaders, and especially by those who have prompted fashion. Indeed, we would not be going too far to maintain that the Jugendstil, through the purely formalistic extravagance and ornamental display that prevailed in its works from the beginning, has actually been conjured up by them. We were and are still today fixed in the ornamental phase of the craft arts; the so-called new ornament has now simply stepped in and replaced the previously fashionable Rococo ornament. Still the concept of ornament prevails everywhere. The arts and crafts are understood simply and exclusively as ornament. Whoever wishes to study the arts and crafts thinks first of the study of ornament. Just as the public limits the concept of art to the painted canvas, so the arts and crafts signify for them ornament.

Yet in the end everyone will understand that ornament and the arts and crafts are not synonymous, that it is a matter of form and not of decoration, and that a form is not to be excluded from the arts and crafts because it is unornamented. The fateful impulse for ornament conjured up the entire contemporary artistic distress.

We may be pleased by ornamental embellishment from the hand of an artist, just as we may love the verse of a poet. But just imagine that the entire world only spoke poetically and our ear heard nothing other than the most hackneyed rhymes. How frightful! And yet the Jugendstil mode of our contemporary arts and crafts represents this phase; that which, burdening our ears, we find horrible, our eyes must suffer daily. All new products brim with ornamental forms. The factories today stamp out Jugendstil ornament just as they previously stamped out Rococo ornament, and hundreds of shops, filled with the most useless odds and ends (knickknacks), bloom and thrive in the propagation of this mischief. If only we could leave them in the shop, where they would then burden only the display window! But with thousands of opportunities—birthday, wedding, and friendship gifts of all kinds—we transport them into the house, where they then still further increase the disarray that, without them, already prevailed in the German interior. Yet this is taken for art. And today everyone cries out for art.

Considering the misjudgment that has for decades driven mankind to a misguided need for art (and now when the surge of the artistic movement goes so high, it even forcefully drives us on again), many already sympathize with the quiet desire to escape from this fatal artistic bustle once and for all. And many perhaps share the feeling that we would be better off if the word *art* and with it the term *arts and crafts*, were for now no more used with regard to our domestic surroundings. The well-being and the hope of the future lies in this: in the conceptual bonding of arts and crafts to subdue "art" in the recovery of a suitable craft production. We talk incessantly about the higher issue of art and have yet to consider the underlying craft aspect of the problem. In the question of the so-called arts and crafts, it is by no means a matter of art but rather of realizing what are the simplest elements underpinning it. Were all the superfluous exaggeration, all the bad taste, all the low quality that today dominate the field and establish the tone for outfitting today's dwelling expelled from the world, then we would perhaps be content to leave art alone. Instead we drag in a so-called art and thus pile evil upon evil.

Contemporary German society is dominated by parvenu pretension and spends its life in a sham culture. When the well-heeled bourgeoisie feels itself somewhat comfortable, it engages in a lively effort to better its appearance and believes to be able to do so above all by sewing on antiquated aristocratic patches. Thus we have our recent dubious achievements in so-called courtly forms: consider only the now generalized "gracious lady," the hand kiss, and so forth. Thus every individual anxiously hopes that others will have a good opinion of him—an effort to which we can trace so many deplorable customs, haughty banquets, the entire style or so-called "fine figure" of so many poor devils, and the total artificiality of our presumed sociableness. Thus we have also the hanging out of titles and superficial badges of rank, and the general aspiration in "higher" circles; and thus we have the barbarism in contemporary dwellings. What would one expect from a culture with so little of its own feeling of personality but that superficial display, that false finery, and that gilded hollow form of today's dwelling? Even here it shines only in false reflection of a world to which it does not belong. What does the burgher have to do with the courtly gilded Rococo chair, with the pompous ceiling, with the marble, symmetrical palace staircase that leads to his spatially modest apartment? All these things are not middle class; they are borrowed from aristocratic culture. In any case they are, one must concede, for the most part suitably made up for their altered use; in material as in production they are now false, that is, assembled out of surrogates, whereas previously they were genuine. And so, as a notable irony of fate, they strikingly represent precisely by their falseness the sentiment for which they were employed. But the innocent user does not notice this. The burgher can discern this falseness no better than he can appreciate an unpretentious breeding of taste or understand the workmanlike and the genuine. Today the factory produces the surrogate with the cheapest machine labor. If it superficially looks the same as the genuine article, why not use it?

MACHINE
SURROGATES It is a common precept that it was the machine in particular that killed both the crafts and the sense for workmanlike authenticity. Nevertheless, we must take care not to regard machine work as necessarily evil and condemn it outright, as the socially concerned English Arts and Crafts Movement has done. To be sure, the machine was harmful in the way it was first used to produce false things, in the way it overstepped the limits of its own domain and cast cheap trash on the market. Artistically, it has till now limited its production almost solely to fakes, and thus for its own part directly contributed to confounding the issue so utterly. It was opportunistic in pressing on pasteboard what was previously carved in wood, in stamping with the steel press that which the goldsmith previously hammered. And it did so extensively. The middle class was satiated with these cheap surrogates; our contemporary dwellings simply burst with them. Indeed, even circles whose tradition should preserve them from such error suffer today from clouded vision—observe the cheap machine rubbish of trimmings and lace, even on the toilette of the aristocratic lady! Taste in consumption, ornament, and display in general has fallen prey to the offering of easily produced, cheap surrogates.

How does machine work differ from handwork? It is a repetition lacking spirit. Ornament made by the human hand carries traces of its production, the artistic impulse of the creator, the delight and sorrow of its achievement, the pleasure of work. Machine work presents of this life only a death mask. And not only this, mass production vulgarizes the earlier individual artistic production, in that to a certain extent it affects the poetic on the street organ. The general resistance to ornament, commonly observed today, perhaps corresponds to this surfeit of machine ornament.

Obviously the machine does not exist in order to produce art. This is a privilege of the human hand; only with our hand are we able to create works that arrest the more intimate interest of our fellows. To this end, the human hand can use tools; human ingenuity depends on their use and the existence of the tool is certainly a given of our culture. The machine is, however, only an improved tool. To exclude it as such from our human production would be foolish, yet it is an equally great error to have it automatically produce things in which we wish to have a personal, spiritual delight, as we have previously had from works of art.

The machine, however, has been misused not only to produce false works of art, it has also introduced a mode of production that aims at mass operation and thus evoked a series of further evils—above all a reciprocal undercutting of prices. Once this principle was in place, it soon became a battle of life and death. Extensive operating equipment consumes interest whenever it is not in operation. Thus it must produce whether the world needs the wares or not. The buyer who has no particular need for them is enticed by their unprecedented cheapness. The necessary condition is only too often the worst quality; this is the result of the pressure on the worker to work ever faster and faster. The buyer purchases in ignorance of the minimal value, about which he is deceived by a pleasing presentation; indeed, he believes by the low price to have obtained an economic advantage. Not only does the lack of durability soon spoil this delusion but defects soon give cause for constant dissatisfaction—if the thing has not already fallen apart. Soon it is thrown away or finds its natural ruin, and a new one must be bought.

MASS PRODUCTION AND ITS RESULTS

What then is the result of this supply of cheap factory goods? The factory worker is forced to earn less in order that the factory can meet the competition; he loses interest in his work and is spiritually injured because he must deliver bad work. An entire class is thus demoralized because the natural human instinct to take pleasure in excellent work is repressed. The buyer is prompted to a false economy in that in a short span of time he must acquire a series of flimsy articles; and the irritating quality of the wares holds him, like the worker, in constant discontent. The national wealth is greatly injured by this, for raw materials, which in part must be imported, are continuously used up in unsatisfactory forms and thus are squandered.

It is thus evident what deep harm today preys upon our trades. The new conditions are not yet understood, not to speak of being controlled. The machine must be, like every improved tool, a blessing rather than a curse for mankind. Its productions need not be inartistic nor without quality. If the human mind simply conceives forms that the machine can produce, then these, as soon as they logically evolve from the conditions of the machine, will also be those that we will without hesitation call artistic. They will satisfy completely so long as they are not fakes of handwork but rather typical machine forms. The bicycle, machine tools, the iron bridge provide pointers. The product of the machine can

THE MACHINE AS TOOL

only be an undecorated practical form [*Sachform*], the particular form that the machine produces best. Man then assembles these forms for human production. He thus thinks at a larger scale and extends the realm of his effectiveness. With the iron bridge it is no longer the angle irons and rivet heads that interest us, as did the hammer strokes of the smithy's work earlier, but rather the bold span, which is simultaneously a representation of the audacity and power of the human spirit.

That the machine need not work without distinction, as until now it has done in part, should be apparent. Demand of it only what it can produce; do not ask it to perform work that must be reserved for the human hand; do not direct it to disgorge cheap, mass trash. It is a tool, not a goddess of production.

THE ENCOURAGEMENT OF QUALITY Obviously it will require the insight and then also the watchful eye of the public to counter the factory owners' tendency to bless the world with their machine-produced trash. Previously the guilds upheld the level of work. With today's altered conditions, the public must be on its guard against the factory owners. This requires a fundamental public education in the appreciation of quality, which today has not even begun. The advancement of genuineness in craft comes before the advancement of art. Indeed, if the many household artifacts that fill our dwellings were simply genuine and of excellent handwork, if all fakery were thoroughly avoided, then we would not need to speak of art at all in order to arrive at a tolerable situation; a certain natural taste would then suffice. And with limitation to simple middle-class motifs and the exclusion of all false pretension, the most primitive claims of taste would suffice. Why do the old rooms of farmers always appear so comfortable? Because for better or worse they embody an unfalsified culture.

The new movement of the arts and crafts will mean nothing for the world if it is not united with a more open, honest public sensibility. Where it would otherwise lead has been shown by the Jugendstil. Everyone desires solid and genuine household artifacts before turning to artistic ones. Our craft will be better enhanced by this than by the frequently encouraged influence of art. Prices would be somewhat higher, but the increased durability would fully compensate for this. Among the workers, ambition and the joy of the matter would be stimulated and thus an entire class would be kept from moral ruin. At the same time it would be possible to increase wages and demand a higher return for quality goods than for trashy wares. Finally, because raw materials would be used in the most rational manner, holes in our national economy, out of which millions of marks flow annually to no purpose, would be plugged. Progress requires that the people again acquire the understanding of quality. Here the state must first enter as teacher because it controls the demand for quality by the products it obtains. It would be particularly appropriate that state and public buildings were brought to the highest quality through the greatest authenticity with tasteful, exemplary character. The highest measure of authenticity would be achieved on principle and completely independent of cost, for the state has the duty above all to serve as a model. Also, by intensifying the requirement for quality it would enhance the national wealth better than by the attempt to save a few thousand marks. This is all the more true in that Germany is extraordinarily backward in advancing quality, more backward than its current national wealth permits. In England every worker knows that he does better to buy a chair for five marks rather than for three; and people who are well off believe that the best is precisely good enough for them. Thus we have all sorts of quality goods in English handicrafts. And thus (an aspect of the matter that must be mentioned) there is the high reputation of English wares throughout the world. In contrast, German goods are burdened with the stain of inferior value, and it will be long before we put aside this prejudice, even with the constant purveying of good products. We ourselves are more or less appraised by our wares. The failing effort to produce quality thus has the most prejudicial national results.

If genuineness and propriety are to be encouraged for our everyday artifacts, then authenticity of form in the conception, material, and production of the arts and crafts is essential—before we can even speak further of raising the object into the realm of art. Artistic enhancement has, however, nothing to do either with the type of ornamentation or with the extent of display, but rather here again a viewpoint must be understood that in the production of the nineteenth century was too often neglected, in part forgotten: the organic relation of the individual object to the artistic whole. In the sense of the arts and crafts the whole can only be the interior understood as a unity. Consequently the person engaged in the arts and crafts is an interior artist. A carpet of however beautiful a pattern or a highly artistic wardrobe has an infinitesimal scope if it does not contribute to the organic structure of the interior. This new understanding is an achievement of the new arts and crafts. It supersedes the earlier viewpoint according to which a room with its content was a hodgepodge of all possible, more or less interesting, individual objects, as we still may observe in the rooms of the museums of applied art. The room of the 1870s and 1880s was itself a small museum of applied art, only filled with fakes instead of the real thing. And generally that remains true today for the typical room not yet reached by the new art movement.

THE NEW SENSE OF THE ARTS AND CRAFTS

Considering that we have had a new movement for almost ten years, the slight influence it has had on the German interior and the German house is surprising. Everyone today cries for artistic culture, even for the children, yet we dwell in a Babylonian confusion.

ART AND LIFE

This is true even for many of the writers who give lectures on aesthetics and write books on art; at home they are surrounded by artistic barbarism. It is also true for architects, who ought to be the qualified representatives of good taste. It is characteristic of the German mind that here, too, the separation of theory and practice is introduced. Art is separated from life; what is espoused or practiced in the office does not affect the way of life. The economic condition is usually offered as an excuse. Yet if we would only decide to take one step out of the extravagantly false culture in which we live, if rather than for others we would only live and dwell for our own sake, then we could with little difficulty overcome that separation of art and life. Taste, moreover, when practiced with a little intelligence, does not cost money. If one observes such falseness even among the young, what can we expect of the old? Under such circumstances, how will we be able to bring about an improvement in the greater public?

SENSATIONAL ART AND MIDDLE-CLASS ART

We also see certain parties, whose intentions must appear doubtful, taking an interest in the new movement—that is, those parties who struggle for the sensational of whatever type and at any price, above all in order to shine before an army of admirers in the pomp of their opulence. They thus encourage that the new art be taken as that *haut goût* and exaggeration of display that until now often struck them so disagreeably. The new art cannot be engaged with such patronage. If it wants to better the world, it must turn to broader circles. Its particular goal can only be our middle class. The wind that today blows across our culture is middle class. Just as today we all work, just as everyone's clothing is middle class, just as our new tectonic forms (insofar as they are not the work of architects) move in the track of complete simplicity and straightforwardness [*Sachlichkeit*], so also we want to live in middle-class rooms whose essence and goal is simplicity and straightforwardness. No limits are set to good taste within these forms of straightforwardness; indeed here it can be engaged more genuinely than in the worn out, ostentatious cramming of our houses today.

ART OF EMOTION AND ART OF THE REAL [*SACHE*]

It is said that only the soft, flowing line, which thus far has principally engaged the new art of the Continent, is in a position to do justice to the finer nuances of the modern, strongly differentiated, emotional life—to capture the fleeting moods that modern man would see embodied in the work of art. Yet an art of feeling, even under the best of conditions, can only correspond with the emotional life of the moment, and we must remain aware that it moves on the shifting ground of constantly changing values. The gravitational axis that lies within the swings of the pendulum of emotional values, which alone within the motion is enduring and mathematically describable, is prescribed for the tectonic arts in the necessary and constant demands of material, function, and construction. The more perfectly these demands are fulfilled, the more lasting will be the values achieved. {The already mentioned emotional whipping of lines does not take into account the material; it forces the ornament of the book, the brass candlestick, and the piece of furniture into exactly the same meanders. With furniture design in particular it demands irresponsible sacrifices in the treatment of construction and material, since the most evident property of wood is the clear directionality of its fibers. And even if today's technology can overcome any difficulty of construction resulting from this approach, and even if we have imported species of woods from overseas that are the most resistant to splitting, the joiner's trade nevertheless works in strongly artificial relations. Aside from all other considerations, these practices are extremely expensive, expensive for impractical [unsachlichen] reasons. Taken very generally, treating a material in a way contrary to its nature is hardly in accord with the spirit of our time, which is characterized by very straightforward [sachlich] and rational thought. The new movement would gain much conviction and popularity if it displayed more naturalness and human understanding. A strong dose of realism would do it enormous good. Then, too, its products would be available to the greater number of the people,} and thus the goal of generalizing the movement would be significantly advanced. What we need is not an emotion-laden furniture and a luxurious art but decent household artifacts for the ordinary man.

In this matter virtually nothing has yet been achieved. The worthwhile has been shown over and over in exhibitions, competitions, and journals; only in the German dwelling does inauthentic display and spurious art still remain in full bloom, as if nothing had happened. Household artifacts are at a level that is deserving of the bad taste of the interior decoration. The gilded Rococo interior with the horrifying stove is now succeeded by the no less gilded and absurd Jugendstil interior. The public, even so-called cultured people, and members of high society, tumble into such dizziness and hold fast for their lives. They are, in fact, comfortable in such an environment because they take it to be art. The nature of our dwellings creates part of the problem. {In contrast to England, where the much older art movement, almost from the beginning, had the opportunity to see its natural base as the house, where through all levels of the society the desire flourished to live in one's own house and to make it a permanent residence—the German has no proper house. Unsettled in a manner that appears to have retained something from nomadic life, he seeks his lodging in the apartment buildings of factorylike production. The slight interest that he attaches to the rooms into which accident has thrust him, and which he changes as lightheartedly as a hotel room, is a deeply rooted cancer of our German art. A change in this situation can only take its start in the German house, which essentially is yet to be created.}

THE RENTAL
DWELLING

If the possibility to live in a single-family house is, on the one hand, economically denied to most (a problem even greater in Germany as we have given land speculation unlimited scope, thereby sapping the vitality of the people), it is incomprehensible, on the other hand, why the majority of those who are well-off stunt themselves in urban flats, instead of living in their own homes. That they choose not to do so simply demonstrates their lack of a sense for home and for dwelling. Yet the future of our artistic culture depends on such a sense. {Art begins, like so much else, at home. Only he who takes an artistic interest in his four walls, who is himself naturally inclined to shape his personal surroundings, will give form to his taste and bring that sensitivity for art from his rooms into the street and the larger environment. And this is imperative if our contemporary world is again to have a broader appreciation of art.}

Above all, our present so very unvernacular architecture cannot succeed to the vernacular except through the study[138] of the domestic building-art. This must first be newly constructed. Even here reform can only proceed from the small to the large, only from the interior to the exterior. Every individual has it in his power to design the room in which he lives in a reasonable, artistic[139] manner. If the sensibility for this is awakened in broader circles, then a more genuine popular feeling for the appearance of the house will necessarily follow. And if this exists, then the individual has the key for understanding architectural questions in general. The building-art will then, perhaps, no longer be for him that insignificant—indeed unfriendly—specialist's art, which it has been up to now for the general public; it will again enter the realm of his understanding and his interest.

This picture of a possible course of events can be documented by an example: development in England began this way, and it has led to a brilliant unfolding of the domestic art. There the Arts and Crafts Movement under William Morris started its reform work in the interior of the house. Before long there followed a total revolution in the domestic building-art. Even in England the building-art had been fettered by an abstract formalism: Gothicists and classicists outbid one another from opposite sides in the most impracticable [*unsachliche*] architecture-mongering. The Gothicists, in the numerous commissions for houses that they received, trotted out small castlelike compositions of inauthentic church forms; the classicists created those stuccoed and oil-painted, roofless boxes, the final modification of the Palazzo Strozzi ideal of which we have sufficient examples in Germany. At this point the new architecture movement began. Its father was the architect Norman Shaw, and it is generally known by the name of Queen Anne.[140] What this movement sought and what then was done have very little to do with Queen Anne. It was nothing other than a rejection of architectural formalism in favor of a simple and natural, reasonable way of building. One brought nothing new to such a movement; everything had existed for centuries in the vernacular architecture of the small town and rural landscape: in those regions of building practice into which the Italian-cultured architect had not ventured, but rather where, in earlier centuries, the country mason had followed local traditions in his practice. Here, amid the architectural extravagance that the architects promoted, one found all that one desired and for which one thirsted: adaptation to needs and local conditions, unpretentiousness and honesty[141] of feeling; utmost coziness and comfort in the layout of rooms, color, an uncommonly attractive and painterly (but also reasonable) design, and an economy in building construction. The new English domestic building-art that developed on this basis has now produced valuable results. But it has also done more: it has spread the interest and the understanding for domestic architecture to the entire people. It has created the only sure foundation for a new artistic culture: the artistic[142] house. And as everyone connected with the Arts and Crafts Movement in England certainly knows, it produced that for which everyone labored: the English house. In contrast, our new Continental movement will have to wander in journals and exhibitions until we Germans will finally have an artistic[143] house.

There is no reason why we should not be able to do in our own way what once was done in England: to return our vernacular building-art to simplicity and naturalness, as is preserved in our old rural buildings; to renounce every architectural trinket on and in our house; and to introduce a sense of spatial warmth, color, natural layout, and sensible configuration instead of continuing to be restrained by the chains of formalistic and academic architecture-mongering. The way in which the English achieved this goal, namely, by readapting vernacular and rural building motifs, promises us the richest harvest—precisely in Germany where the rural building manner of the past is clothed in a poetry and a wealth of sentiment that few old English buildings can match. If we restrict ourselves to the homegrown, and if each of us impartially follows his own individual artistic inclinations, then we will soon have not only a reasonable but also a national, vernacular building-art. Nationality in art need not be artificially bred. If one raises genuine people, we will have a genuine art that for every individual with a sincere character can be nothing other than national. For every genuine person is a part of a genuine nationality.

POSSIBILITIES IN GERMANY

Obviously this entails divesting ourselves of the tendencies associated with our youthful middle-class culture, which we now encounter all too often. These are our attempts to show off as much as possible, to impress our neighbors, and to shine outwardly through ostentatious expenditure. It is precisely these tendencies that today make the architectural character of German cities so unpleasant, as we see, for example, in Berlin, which has boomed at an American tempo. It is also these tendencies that have produced the frequently encountered yearning of German clients to see their middle-class home built in the manner of the palazzo of an Italian Renaissance prince. Without stripping away such false sensibilities, we shall not arrive at a natural and healthy, artistic condition.[144] A genuine art can only rest on genuine feelings. Art is not solely a matter of ability and the exercise of aesthetic feelings but, above all else, a matter of character and sensibility. They must be maintained especially in architecture, the art of daily life. Every disregard of the straightforward [*sachlichen*] goal, every surrender to farfetched viewpoints must be most bitterly avenged—as bitterly as we have seen the building-art of the last century reduced to "style-architecture."

RESULTS AND HOPES

Among all consequences of the diverse architectural changes of the nineteenth century, perhaps the most important is the beginning of a new perspective on the question of style. The century that is most clearly marked architecturally by the chaotic confusion of all past styles has at least yielded one thing: a complete devaluation of this style instinct. Today we no longer consider the mere academic use of a historic architectural style to be a merit. Indeed, it hardly elicits our interest. It is now out of the question that any of the readopted old architectural styles could present itself as the contemporary style, or that any could be shown to be vital. Even the mighty attempts to invent a new style through outside means have led to nothing precisely because they remain superficial. The enormous expenditure and expansion of the limits of aesthetics and archaeology in the last century, the desparate efforts of entire schools of philosophy to assist artistic creation with rules—these have had no effect on the ever more diseased body of architecture. Like someone treated with false medicines, its vital forces have convulsed all the more.

While Mother Architecture found herself on a wrong path, life never rested but went on to create forms for the innovations it had produced, the simple forms of pure practicality [*Sachlichkeit*]. It created our machines, vehicles, implements, iron bridges, and glass halls. It led the way soberly in that it proceeded practically— one would like to say purely scientifically. It not only embodied the spirit of the time but also fitted itself to the aesthetic-tectonic views that were reformed under the same influence. These views, ever more decisively than the earlier decorative art, demanded a corresponding, straightforward [*sachlich*] art.

The unclarified romantic efforts, insofar as they were architecturally expressed, already sought a straightforward [*sachlich*] art. It was most significant that this Romantic Movement, for the first time in the nineteenth century, returned to those Nordic views of art that were essentially pragmatic [*sachlich*] and constructional, as was embodied with such great clarity in Gothic art. The great process of reform weakened only because the Neogothic school, like the classicists, degenerated into the superficial and formal, into a mere stylistic conception. Yet despite all the waverings and fermentations in the nineteenth century, it began to mature with increasing consistency: the substitution of the classic ideal of beauty by a new one corresponding to the Nordic-Germanic spirit.

If one would characterize both ideals in words, one could say that the art of the Latin peoples strives for a formal beauty that is considered universally valid, whereas the Germanic peoples seek the characteristic, the individual. Instead of the classical and Italian conception of art as a harmony concealing essence, the Nordic people prefer to emphasize the characteristic feature of the special conditions. Instead of the accepted outward lines of beauty, we seek the inwardly pleasing; instead of the symmetrical, we seek the form fitted to the circumstances; instead of the pathetic, we seek the reasonable. Classic art is the art of the universal; Germanic art is that of the particular.[145]

In this individualism, the German conception of art approaches that which we currently designate, in the best sense, as the modern. It is also consonant with the new viewpoint of architectural design discussed above,[146] in which the achievements of past architecture are placed in the service of a personal design, one adapted to every purpose and emotional goal. Likewise we have the now-apparent need to acknowledge the special attributes of a building, to characterize the particular kind of space architecturally. This spirit is in full accord with the underlying realistic tendency, as well as with the motifs of mood and individuality in[147] the new Arts and Crafts Movement. Moreover, it has a distinct Germanic coloration in that it was developed by Nordic peoples, and up till now has been almost exclusively limited to them. Parallel efforts are to be found in the other arts: the changes in painting and poetry, from naturalism on the one hand to emotional values on the other,[148] point to the same goal.

Today our goal in art must be sought in the integration of all these vacillating movements of the present, with a clearer awareness of their collective center of gravity. For there are no special arts, only a great universal art. It is an indication of its vigor that it represents[149] a single conviction. Architecture, as the most difficult of the arts, will naturally be the last to be in a position to draw the full consequences of the new spirit. But the new movement in the arts and crafts has prepared new powers for it. Notwithstanding all errors and occasional derailments, we can still say that its sound core has approached the artistic questions of the time very broadly, such that with a further clarification of its goals it may provide the transition to a timely reform of our tectonic activity. Already a community of adherents has congregated around the new ideas. The leaders of the movement have already engaged in a pioneering work that history will perhaps recognize as a great feat. The way to further development is smoothed. As the bearer of the new ideas, a new spiritual aristocracy arises, which this time stems from the best of the middle class rather than the hereditary aristocratic elements, and this especially clearly signals the new and enlarged goal of the movement: the creation of a contemporary middle-class art. A strong artistic current, unimaginable ten years ago, streams through the German heart, and a deep desire for a purer state of art moves the whole of Germany. Now it is important for those neophytes to stand fast and not be led into error by the whims of fashion. The goal remains sincerity, straightforwardness [*Sachlichkeit*], and a purity of artistic sensibility, qualities that avoid all secondary considerations and superficialities, so that one can be fully dedicated to the great problem of the time. **But architecture must be resolved to do this**[150] **if she is to reconquer the position due to her in the concert of the arts. If from the labyrinth of the arts of the last hundred years we are ever again to succeed to artistic conditions that bear even a remote similarity to the great epochs of the history of art, then architecture must assume leadership in the community of the arts. From her must come the rays of a new artistic life. She will be the one that gives the other arts a spine and breathes into them again the grandeur and firmness that they possessed under her leadership in earlier periods of brilliance.**

Ruskin, the artistic apostle of England, felt this when he wrote at the end of the 1840s: "I believe architecture must be the beginning of arts, and that the others must follow her in their time and order; and I think the prosperity of our schools of painting and sculpture . . . depends upon that of our architecture. I think that all will languish until that takes the lead."[151]

W̶hen will our architecture be ready to assume this responsibility?

In any case, no sooner than when she has arisen to a new golden freedom, free from the stylistic chains in which she has lain bound for a century; no sooner than when she leaves behind a shadowy style-architecture and becomes again a living building-art.

TRANSLATOR'S NOTES

1. In the second edition, Muthesius changed his subtitle to *Wandlungen der Architektur und der gewerblichen Künste im neunzehnten Jahrhundert und ihr heutiger Standpunkt* (Transformations of architecture and industrial arts in the nineteenth century and their present condition).

2. Deleted in the second edition.

3. Address at the Distribution of Prizes at Birmingham, 1894. First published by Longmans, Green & Co. of London in June 1898. Included in volume 22 of *The Collected Works of William Morris* (New York: Russell & Russell, 1966), 429–30.

4. All marginal headings appeared only in the second edition and are thus rendered consistently in the nonbold typeface used throughout to indicate additions made in the second edition.

5. Variation: "rule that prevailed until."

6. Deletion.

7. Variation: "German."

8. Variation: changed from "*hereingebrochen*" to "*gekommen.*"

9. Variation: changed from "*zum Ausgang einer Namengebung wählen*" to "*für eine Namengebung wählen.*"

10. Deletion.

11. Variation: "the universal Gothic art."

12. Deletion.

13. The concepts embodied in the word *Sachlichkeit* and its adjectival form, *sachlich*, are central to Muthesius's argument in *Stilarchitektur*. While an English translation is offered each time these German words appear, the choice is always somewhat inadequate. The Introduction attempts to build a nuanced view of the use of these words at the turn of the century. Please refer to note 10 of the Introduction (p. 38) for more information regarding the handling of these terms throughout the present volume.

14. The section break following this sentence does not appear in the second edition.

15. James Stuart (1713–1788) and Nicholas Revett (1720–1804): *The Antiquities of Athens*, 4 vols. (London, 1762–1814; reprint, New York: Arno, 1968).

16. Johann Joachim Winckelmann (1717–1768): *Geschichte der Kunst des Altertums* (Dresden: Walther, 1764); translated by G. H. Lodge as *The History of Ancient Art* (Boston: Little Brown [vol. 1], 1856; J. Munroe [vol. 2], 1849; J. R. Osgood [vols. 3, 4], 1872–1875; reprint, New York: F. Ungar, 1968).

17. Variation: "badly chosen."

18. Karl Friedrich Schinkel (1781–1841). Variation: this phrase is a separate sentence.

19. Ludwig I of Bavaria (1786–1868).

20. Leo von Klenze (1784–1864).

21. Theophil von Hansen (1813–1891).

22. Deletion of the quotation marks surrounding "scientific explanation."

23. Carl Bötticher (1806–1899): *Die Tektonik der Hellenen* (Potsdam: F. Riegel, 1844–1852; 2nd ed., 2 vols. plus atlas, Berlin: Ernst & Korn, 1874).

24. Variation: "feelings."

25. Ludwig Persius (1803–1845); Friedrich August Stüler (1800–1865); Johann Heinrich Strack (1805–1880).

26. Friedrich Hitzig (1811–1881); Richard Lucae (1829–1877); Martin Gropius (1824–1880).

27. Heino Schmieden (1835–1913).

28. Charles Percier (1764–1838); Pierre-François-Léonard Fontaine (1762–1853).

29. Jean-François-Thérèse Chalgrin (1739–1811).

30. Pierre Vignon (1763–1828).

31. Jean-Louis-Charles Garnier (1825–1898).

32. Joseph Poelaert (1817–1879).

33. Inigo Jones (1573–1652).

34. Adam brothers: Robert (1728–1792) and James (1732–1794).

35. Henry William Inwood (1794–1843).

36. Sir John Soane (1753–1837).

37. Variation: "special finery."

38. Variation: no paragraph break.

39. Variation: "was no longer the source of."

40. Variation: The section break following this sentence does not appear in the second edition.

41. Deletion.

42. Variation: "fulfills a."

43. Variation: "an important."

44. Deletion.

45. Variation: "their historical value has been denied."

46. Friedrich von Gärtner (1792–1847).

47. Conrad Wilhelm Hase (1818–1902); Georg Gottlob Ungewitter (1820–1864).

48. Deletion. Johannes Otzen (1839–1911).

49. *"Protestantischer Kirchenbau."*

50. Variation: "corresponded with."

51. Heinrich von Ferstel (1828–1883).

52. Friedrich von Schmidt (1825–1891).

53. Variation: "work whose worth extends." Changes in this paragraph amount to a diminished appreciation of Schmidt's Rathaus.

54. Eugène-Emmanuel Viollet-le-Duc (1814–1879): *Dictionnaire raisonné de l'architecture*

française du XIe au XVIe siècle (Paris: Morel, 1875); idem, *Entretiens sur l'architecture* (Paris: Morel, 1863–1872).

55. Léon Vaudoyer (1803–1872); Paul Abadie (1813–1884).

56. Sir Walter Scott (1771–1832).

57. Sir Charles Barry (1795–1860); Augustus Welby Northmore Pugin (1812–1852).

58. George Gilbert Scott (1811–1878); George Street (1824–1881); John Loughborough Pearson (1817–1897).

59. Deletion.

60. William Morris (1834–1896).

61. John Ruskin (1819–1900).

62. Karl Schaefer (1844–1908).

63. Variation: "provided the standard."

64. Deletion.

65. Variation: "no longer."

66. Walter Kyllmann (1837–1913); Adolf Heyden (1838–1902); Hermann Ende (1829–1907); Wilhelm Böckmann (1832–1902); Karl von Hasenauer (1833–1894); Christian Leins (1814–1892).

67. Gottfried Semper (1803–1879): *Der Stil in den technischen und tektonischen Künsten; oder, Praktische Ästhetik*, 2 vols. (Munich: F. Bruckmann, 1860–1863; 2nd ed., Munich: F. Bruckmann, 1878–1879; reprint, Mittenwald: Maeander Kunstverlag, 1977).

68. Variation: "tectonic arts."

69. Variation: changed from "*Kunstgewerbetreibende*" to "*Kunstgewerbler.*"

70. Variation: "learned."

71. Variation: "will."

72. Variation: "transport."

73. Sir Joseph Paxton (1801–1865).

74. Pierre-François-Henri Labrouste (1801–1875).

75. Alfred Messel (1853–1909).

76. Variation: "halls."

77. Deletion.

78. Deletion.

79. Variation: "formative."

80. Deletion.

81. Paul Wallot (1841–1912).

82. Variation: "one of the few figures."

83. Variation: "curse."

84. Variation: "made."

85. Variation: "one automatically observed a distinction between a monumental building-art and a middle-class building-art."

86. Variation: "that met one's everyday needs in dwellings and minor buildings."

87. Variation: "general."

88. Deletion.

89. Deletion.

90. Variation: "that offend no less through the frivolous, parvenu sensibility with which they are stamped than in the rapture of the unnecessary and the senseless with which they are burdened. Alongside these, the older buildings of the inner city touch us like a redemption. Here we still confront manifestations of the old, unfalsified guild tradition that, in their simple demeanor, stand out today as the witnesses of a golden age in the degenerate present."

91. Deletion.

92. Variation: "spatially or temporally."

93. Variation: "—men from whose artistic sensibility we are today far distant. There is indeed already a chasm that separates us from the generation of twenty years ago!"

94. Variation: "imputed to."

95. Variation: "variety."

96. Variation: "had been laid on mankind in the form of classicism."

97. Deletion.

98. Variation: "Now people split into parties for the various styles; classicists and romantics feuded among themselves for decades."

99. Variation: "not."

100. Maximilian II (1811–1864).

101. Deletion.

102. Variation: "still more perhaps in those forms that fall completely outside the realm of activity of the architect, thus so to say, sprout wild, as."

103. Deletion.

104. Variation: "that was hit upon precisely according to."

105. Variation: "born of our most particular time, there must be."

106. Deletion.

107. Variation: "decoratively carved sedan chair the Rococo period."

108. Variation: "as the dress of the nobleman, still in the second half of the eighteenth century."

109. Variation: "also in no way consists strictly of utilitarian elements."

110. Variation: "that aims not only to hinder undesired accumulations of dirt but also wants always."

111. Variation: "In this demand our starched white linens also find their justification."

112. Variation: "is also to be recognized."

113. Variation: "replace the heavy and unmovable with light."

114. Variation: "sharp boundaries cannot be drawn. Closed form cannot be separated from monumental building-art."

115. Variation: "verse; to desire a realistic design that is strictly fitted to need would here be an error."

116. Variation: "Chiefly responsible for this are the superficial style movements that during the entire recent development weighed heavily upon it."

117. Sentence break.

118. Variation: the introductory phrase "If he builds" replaces the "In the first case" of the first edition.

119. Variation: "proffered."

120. Variation: "stylistic."

121. Variation from "*Architektur*" to "*Stilarchitektur*," although the original was also clearly meant to be critical and dismissive.

122. Variation: "number of."

123. Variation: "A."

124. Variation: "Even over this narrower Arts and Crafts Movement obviously no definitive judgment can be made. The movement in Germany presented itself until now as a bubbling brew of often antagonistic ingredients, which was far from presenting a united image—and still today that which is in any case satisfying must be sought more in its program than in the general norm of its production."

125. Variation: "Where it most differs is in the luxuriant extravagance of form and in the rage for sensational designs—forms that never existed before—which until now could be observed in it."

126. Variation: "create."

127. Variation: "closely."

128. Variation: "join in the expectation."

129. Deletion.

130. There is no paragraph break here in the second edition.

131. Variation: "definitely encouraging."

132. Variation: "form-giving."

133. Variation: "designing."

134. Major variation. The remainder of this paragraph and the next three paragraphs of this first edition text are replaced, in the second edition, by thirty paragraphs that begin—as they do in this translation—with the heading "The New Interior" (see p. 85). The thirty paragraphs of the second-edition text are thus largely new, but they do incorporate, with variations, some parts of the first-edition text. These retained passages are indicated in the translation with brackets of this type { }. Following the thirty new paragraphs, the second edition text resumes with only minor variations on the first edition; see p. 96.

135. What follows here are the thirty new paragraphs added in the second edition (see note 134, above). This addition is preceded by the transitional text that appears on p. 84, prior to note

134. The sentences in brackets { } are slight variants of passages in the first edition that were retained within the longer text of the second edition.

136. James Abbott McNeill Whistler (1834–1903).

137. Henry van de Velde (1863–1957).

138. Variation: "means."

139. Variation: "and tasteful."

140. Richard Norman Shaw (1831–1912).

141. Deletion.

142. Variation: "a national."

143. Deletion.

144. Deletion.

145. Deletion and no paragraph break.

146. Deletion.

147. Variation: "innermost vital core of."

148. Deletion.

149. Variation: "is borne by."

150. Variation: "Architecture must be resolved to join in this spirit."

151. John Ruskin, *The Seven Lamps of Architecture* (London: Smith, Elder, and Co., 1849), 194. In the first edition, but not the second, the next (last) two paragraphs are set off with extra space.

BIBLIOGRAPHY

1891

"Deutsche evangelische Kirche in Tokio." *Centralblatt der Bauverwaltung* 11 (1891): 337–39.

1893

"Ist die Architektur eine Kunst oder ein Gewerbe." *Centralblatt der Bauverwaltung* 13 (1893): 333–35 [review of T. G. Jackson and Richard Norman Shaw, eds. *Architecture a Profession or an Art: Thirteen Short Essays on the Qualifications and Training of Architects*. London: John Murray, 1892].

"Die künstlerische Erziehung der deutschen Jugend." *Centralblatt der Bauverwaltung* 13 (1893): 527–28 [review of Konrad Lange. *Die künstlerische Erziehung der deutschen Jugend*. Darmstadt: Arnold Bergstraßer, 1893].

1894

"Die Architektur auf der Großen Berliner Kunstausstellung." *Centralblatt der Bauverwaltung* 14 (1894): 256–59, 329–30, 335–36, 338–41.

"Deutsche Architekten." *Centralblatt der Bauverwaltung* 14 (1894): 260.

"Das 'Imperial Institute' in London." *Centralblatt der Bauverwaltung* 14 (1894): 149–52, 157.

"Die Preisbewerbung um Entwürfe für ein Rathaus in Elberfeld." *Centralblatt der Bauverwaltung* 14 (1894): 69–70, 79–82, 89–92, 100–102, 114–15.

"Das Urtheil eines Wiener Kunstgelehrten über das deutsche Reichstagsgebäude." *Centralblatt der Bauverwaltung* 14 (1894): 439–40.

1895

"Die Architektur auf der Berliner Kunstausstellung 1895." *Centralblatt der Bauverwaltung* 15 (1895): 350–52.

"Die deutschen Bildsäulen-Denkmale des xix. Jahrhunderts." *Centralblatt der Bauverwaltung* 15 (1895): 43 [review of Hermann Maertens. *Die deutschen Bildsäulen-Denkmale des xix. Jahrhunderts*. Stuttgart: Julius Hoffmann, 1894].

"Das neue Lagerhaus in Worms und die dortigen neueren Baubestrebungen." *Centralblatt der Bauverwaltung* 15 (1895): 117–19, 129–30.

"Das neue Reichsgerichtsgebäude in Leipzig." *Centralblatt der Bauverwaltung* 15 (1895): 449–52, 458–60, 500–501, 521–22.

"Die Preisbewerbung um ein Bismarck-Denkmal für Berlin." *Centralblatt der Bauverwaltung* 15 (1895): 287–88.

"Das Volkshaus in Bishopsgate in London." *Centralblatt der Bauverwaltung* 15 (1895): 77–80.

"Der Wettbewerb um Entwürfe für ein Rathaus in Stuttgart." *Centralblatt der Bauverwaltung* 15 (1895): 277, 282–84, 295–96, 301–3, 321–24.

1896

Muthesius, Hermann, August Endell, and Herman Frobenius. "Krankenhäuser." In *Der Hochbau*, 420–54. Vol. 2 of *Berlin und seine Bauten*. Berlin: Wilhelm Ernst & Sohn, 1896. Reprint. Berlin: Wilhelm Ernst & Sohn, 1988.

1897

"Die Ausbildung der englischen Architekten." *Centralblatt der Bauverwaltung* 17 (1897): 446–48, 459–61.

"Die bakteriologische Klärung der Abwässer in England." *Centralblatt der Bauverwaltung* 17 (1897): 453–56.

"Der Blackwall-Tunnel unter der Themse in London." *Centralblatt der Bauverwaltung* 17 (1897): 239.

"Der englische Ingenieur-Verein (Institution of Civil Engineers) in London." *Centralblatt der Bauverwaltung* 17 (1897): 280.

"Ein englisches Werk über moderne Theater." *Centralblatt der Bauverwaltung* 17 (1897): 471–73.

"Die Eröffnung des Blackwall-Tunnels in London." *Centralblatt der Bauverwaltung* 17 (1897): 246–48.

"John L. Pearson †." *Centralblatt der Bauverwaltung* 17 (1897): 580.

"Die Kathedrale von Peterborough und die Denkmalpflege in England." *Centralblatt der Bauverwaltung* 17 (1897): 164–66.

"Unverbrennbares Holz." *Centralblatt der Bauverwaltung* 17 (1897): 310–11.

"Die Wasserversorgung Londons." *Centralblatt der Bauverwaltung* 17 (1897): 188–89.

"William Morris und die fünfte Ausstellung des Kunstgewerbe-Ausstellungs vereins in London." *Centralblatt der Bauverwaltung* 17 (1897): 3–5, 29–30, 39–41.

1898

"The Architectural Review for the Artist and Craftsman." *Centralblatt der Bauverwaltung* 18 (1898): 11–12 [journal review article].

"Ausstellungen in London." *Dekorative Kunst* 2 (1898): 236–39.

"Ein englisches Werk über moderne Theater." *Centralblatt der Bauverwaltung* 18 (1898): 602–3 [review of Edwin O. Sachs. *Modern Opera Houses and Theatres*. London: B. T. Batsford, 1896–1898].

"Das Feuer in der City von London vom 19. November 1897." *Centralblatt der Bauverwaltung* 18 (1898): 129–31.

"Das Gerichtsgebäude in Birmingham und die neuere Terracotta-Bauweise in England." *Centralblatt der Bauverwaltung* 18 (1898): 265–66, 277–80.

"Die 'Guild and School of Handicraft' in London." *Dekorative Kunst* 2 (1898): 41–48.

"Italienische Reiseeindrücke." *Centralblatt der Bauverwaltung* 18 (1898): 378–80, 386–88, 393–95, 423–25, 433–35, 445–47.

Italienische Reise-Eindrücke. Berlin: Wilhelm Ernst & Sohn, 1898 [originally published in *Centralblatt der Bauverwaltung* 18 (1898)].

"Die Jubiläumsausstellung in London." *Dekorative Kunst* 1 (1898): 208–10.

"Künstlerischer Unterricht für Handwerker in England." *Dekorative Kunst* 1 (1898): 15–20.

"Die neuzeitliche Ziegelbauweise in England." *Centralblatt der Bauverwaltung* 18 (1898): 581–83, 593–95, 605–7, 622–23.

"Die öffentliche Ausstellung der Leiche Gladstones." *Centralblatt der Bauverwaltung* 18 (1898): 295–96.

1899

"Der britische Feuerschutzverein (British Fire Prevention Committee)." *Centralblatt der Bauverwaltung* 19 (1899): 151–52.

"Englische Architektur: 1. Die Arbeiterhäuser in Port Sunlight bei Liverpool." *Dekorative Kunst* 4 (1899): 43–44, 75–77.

"Die englische Bewegung gegen die Ausschreitungen des Ankündigungswesens." *Centralblatt der Bauverwaltung* 19 (1899): 349–51.

"Das englische Haus auf der Pariser Weltausstellung 1900." *Centralblatt der Bauverwaltung* 19 (1899): 284–85.

"Englische und kontinentale Nutzkunst." *Kunst und Handwerk* 49, no. 12 (1899): 321–28.

"Das Fabrikdorf Port Sunlight bei Liverpool." *Centralblatt der Bauverwaltung* 19 (1899): 133–36, 146–48.

"Die Glasfenster Oscar Paterson's in Glasgow." *Dekorative Kunst* 3 (1899): 150–51.

"Das Hauptpolizeigebäude von London (New Scotland Yard)." *Centralblatt der Bauverwaltung* 19 (1899): 317–20.

"Im Kampfe um die Kunst." *Centralblatt der Bauverwaltung* 19 (1899): 372 [review of Fritz Schumacher. *Im Kampfe um die Kunst: Beiträge zu architektonischen Zeitfragen.* Strasbourg: J. H. Ed. Heitz, 1899].

"Der neuere protestantische Kirchenbau in England." *Zeitschrift für Bauwesen* 49 (1899): 361–402, 485–554.

"Die neuzeitliche Ziegelbauweise in England." *Centralblatt der Bauverwaltung* 19 (1899): 7.

1900

"Ein Aachener Patricierhaus des 18. Jahrhunderts." *Die Denkmalpflege* 2 (1900): 128 [review of M. Schmid. *Ein Aachener Patricierhaus des 18. Jahrhunderts.* Stuttgart: J. Hoffman, 1900].

"Amtliche Untersuchungen über Eisenbahnunfälle in England." *Centralblatt der Bauverwaltung* 20 (1900): 55–56.

Architektonische Zeitbetrachtungen: Ein Umblick an der Jahrhundertwende. Berlin: Wilhelm Ernst & Sohn, 1900 [speech given at the Architekten-Verein, Berlin, on 13 March 1900, the occasion of the Schinkelfest. Also published in *Centralblatt der Bauverwaltung* 20 (1900): 125–28, 145–47].

"Die Ausstellungsbauten der Pariser Weltausstellung." *Centralblatt der Bauverwaltung* 20 (1900): 357–58, 371–74, 381–84.

"Die beiden Kunstpaläste der Pariser Weltausstellung." *Centralblatt der Bauverwaltung* 20 (1900): 317–20, 348–49.

"Der Einzelne und seine Kunst." *Centralblatt der Bauverwaltung* 20 (1900): 509 [review of Robert Mielke. *Der Einzelne und seine Kunst.* Leipzig: Georg Heinrich Meyer, 1900].

"Englische Architektur: Ernest Newton." *Dekorative Kunst* 3 (1900): 248–56 [also published in *Die Kunst* 2 (1900)].

"Englische Architektur: George Walton's Innenausbau." *Dekorative Kunst* 3 (1900): 132–34 [also published in *Die Kunst* 2 (1900)].

"Englische Architektur: M. H. Baillie Scott." *Dekorative Kunst* 3 (1900): 5–7 [also published in *Die Kunst* 2 (1900)].

Die Englische Baukunst der Gegenwart: Beispiele neuer Englischer Profanbauten. Leipzig and Berlin: Cosmos, 1900.

"John Ruskin †." *Centralblatt der Bauverwaltung* 20 (1900): 43–44.

"Der Kampf um die neue Kunst." *Centralblatt der Bauverwaltung* 20 (1900): 29–30 [review of Karl Neumann. *Der Kampf um die neue Kunst.* Berlin: Hermann Walther, 1897].

"Die kleineren Bauwerke der Pariser Weltaustellung." *Centralblatt der Bauverwaltung* 20 (1900): 429–32, 441–44.

Der kunstgewerbliche Dilettantismus in England, insbesondere das Wirken des Londoner Vereins für häusliche Kunstindustrie. Berlin: Wilhelm Ernst & Sohn, 1900 [expanded from the original journal article, which appeared in *Centralblatt der Bauverwaltung* 20 (1900)].

"Die 'künstlerischen Thesen' der Vereinigung Berliner Architekten." *Deutsche Bauzeitung* 34 (1900): 438–44.

"Der monumentale Eingang zum Weltausstellungsgelände in Paris." *Centralblatt der Bauverwaltung* 20 (1900): 269–70.

"Die neuen Ministerialgebäude in London." *Centralblatt der Bauverwaltung* 20 (1900): 81.

"Der neuere protestantische Kirchenbau in England." *Zeitschrift für Bauwesen* 50 (1900): 301–44, 455–92.

"Die sechste kunstgewerbliche Ausstellung (Arts and Crafts Exhibition) in New Gallery,

Regent Street, London." *Kunstgewerbeblatt*, n.s., 11 (1900): 141–52.

"Der Sitzungssaal des englischen Unterhauses." *Centralblatt der Bauverwaltung* 20 (1900): 471–72.

"Die Überraschungen Englands." *Tägliche Rundschau* 6 (1900): 21.

"Über unsere häusliche Baukunst." *Deutsche Kunst und Dekoration* 6 (1900): 332–44, 377–84.

"Die vereinigten Müllverbrennungs- und Elektricitätswerke, Bade-, Waschanstalt und Volks- bücherei der Bezirksgemeinde Shoreditch in London." *Centralblatt der Bauverwaltung* 20 (1900): 74–76, 85–88.

"Der 'Verein für häusliche Kunstindustrie' (Home Arts and Industries Association) und der Dilettantismus in den Kleinkünsten in England." *Centralblatt der Bauverwaltung* 20 (1900): 165–67, 173–74, 197–99, 209–12.

"Die Wasserversorgung Londons." *Centralblatt der Bauverwaltung* 20 (1900): 114–15.

"Der Zeichenunterricht in den Londoner Volksschulen." *Pädagogische Blätter für Lehrerbil- dung und Lehrerbildungsanstalten* 29 (1900): 157–71 [also published in *Beiträge zur Lehrerbildung und Lehrerfortbildung* 16 (1900)].

"Zeichenunterricht und 'Stillehre.'" *Die Kunst für Alle* 15 (1900): 487–96 [also published in *Die Kunst* 1 (1900)].

1901

"Die Arbeiterwohnungs-Politik des Londoner Grafschaftsrathes." *Centralblatt der Bauverwal- tung* 21 (1901): 398–401.

"Der Ausbau des Netzes elektrischer Tiefbahnen unter der Stadt London." *Centralblatt der Bau- verwaltung* 21 (1901): 613–16.

"Cremer u. Wolffenstein." *Centralblatt der Bauverwaltung* 21 (1901): 172 [review of Wilhelm Hubert Cremer and Richard Wolffenstein, eds. *Laden- und Geschäftseinrichtungen*. Vol. 3 of *Der innere Ausbau*. Berlin: Ernst Wasmuth, 1900].

"Dante Gabriel Rossetti." *Kunst und Kunsthandwerk* 4 (1901): 373–89.

"Denkmalschutz und Denkmalpflege in England." *Die Denkmalpflege* 3 (1901): 52–54.

"Deutsche Bildhauerkunst im 13. Jahrhundert." *Centralblatt der Bauverwaltung* 21 (1901): 242–44 [review of Maximilian Hasak. *Geschichte der Deutschen Bildhauerkunst im 13. Jahrhundert*. Berlin: Ernst Wasmuth, 1899].

"England." In Richard Graul, ed. *Die Krisis im Kunstgewerbe: Studien über die Wege und Ziele der modernen Richtung*. Part 1, "Betrachtungen über die Entstehung und die Entwick- lung der neuen Richtung in verschiedenen Ländern," 1–20. Leipzig: S. Herzel, 1901.

"Englische Innenkunst auf der Pariser Weltausstellung." *Dekorative Kunst* 4 (1901): 17–30 [also published in *Die Kunst* 4 (1901)].

"Geschäfts- und Warenhäuser." *Centralblatt der Bauverwaltung* 21 (1901): 172 [review of *Ge- schäfts- und Warenhäuser*. Berlin: Ernst Wasmuth, 1898].

"Gleeson White." *Dekorative Kunst* 4 (1901): 66–74 [also published in *Die Kunst* 4 (1901)].

"Die Internationale Ausstellung in Glasgow 1901." *Centralblatt der Bauverwaltung* 21 (1901): 445–48.

"Die Internationale Ausstellung in Glasgow." *Dekorative Kunst* 4 (1901): 489–96 [also published in *Die Kunst* 4 (1901)].

"Krefelder Künstlerseide." *Dekorative Kunst* 4 (1901): 477–85 [also published in *Die Kunst* 4 (1901)].

"Die moderne Bewegung." *Spemanns goldenes Buch der Kunst: Eine Hauskunde für Jederman,* nos. 1029–1066. Berlin and Stuttgart: W. Spemann, 1901.

"Die neue Gemäldegalerie in Whitechapel in London und die volksthümlichen Kunstausstellungen im Londoner Osten." *Centralblatt der Bauverwaltung* 21 (1901): 316–18.

Die neuere kirchliche Baukunst in England: Entwicklung, Bedingungen und Grundzüge des Kirchenbaues der englischen Staatskirche und der Secten. Berlin: Wilhelm Ernst & Sohn, 1901.

"Neues Ornament und neue Kunst." *Dekorative Kunst* 4 (1901): 349–66 [also published in *Die Kunst* 4 (1901)].

"Ruskin in Deutscher Übersetzung." *Centralblatt der Bauverwaltung* 21 (1901): 219–21 [review of John Ruskin. *Die sieben Leuchter der Baukunst, aus dem Englischen von Wilhelm Schoelermann.* Vol. 1 of *Ausgewählte Werke in vollständiger Uebersetzung.* Leipzig: Eugen Diederichs, 1900].

"Stonehenge." *Die Denkmalpflege* 3 (1901): 67–70.

"Die Vorarbeiten für ein Denkmal der Königin Victoria in London." *Centralblatt der Bauverwaltung* 21 (1901): 352–53.

"Der Wettbewerb für das Denkmal der Königin Victoria in London." *Centralblatt der Bauverwaltung* 21 (1901): 585–87.

1902

"Die Architekten Johann Josef Couven und Jakob Couven." *Die Denkmalpflege* 4 (1902): 48 [review of Josef Buchkremer. *Die Architekten Johann Josef Couven und Jakob Couven.* Aachen: Cremersche Buchhandlung, 1896].

"Die Ausstellung der Darmstädter Künstler-Kolonie." *Deutsche Monatsschrift für das gesamte Leben der Gegenwart* 2 (1902): 744–48.

"Das Bauschaffen der Jetztzeit und historische Überlieferung." *Centralblatt der Bauverwaltung* 22 (1902): 72 [review of Fritz Schumacher. *Das Bauschaffen der Jetztzeit und historische Überlieferung.* Leipzig: Eugen Diederichs, 1901].

"Benson's elektrische Beleuchtungskörper." *Dekorative Kunst* 5 (1902): 105–10 [also published in *Die Kunst* 6 (1902)].

"Der Betrieb von Schankwirthschaften durch gemeinnützige Gesellschaften in England." *Centralblatt der Bauverwaltung* 22 (1902): 67–70.

"Einige örtliche Bedingungen der Hausanlage in England." *Centralblatt der Bauverwaltung* 22 (1902): 475–76.

"Die Glasgower Kunstbewegung: Charles R. Mackintosh und Margaret Macdonald-Macintosh." *Dekorative Kunst* 5 (1902): 193–217 [also published in *Die Kunst* 6 (1902)]

"Kulturarbeiten. 1. Bd.: Hausbau. 2. Bd.: Gärten." *Centralblatt der Bauverwaltung* 22 (1902): 641 [review of Paul Schultze-Naumberg. *Kulturarbeiten.* 2 vols. Munich: G. D. W. Callwey, 1902–].

"Kunst für die Armen." *Dekorative Kunst* 5 (1902): 52–57 [also published in *Die Kunst* 6 (1902)].

"Kunst und Leben in England." *Zeitschrift für bildende Kunst* 37, n.s., 13 (1902): 13–21, 49–69; 38, n.s. 14 (1903): 25–43, 73–84.

"Kunst und Maschine." *Dekorative Kunst* 5 (1902): 141–47 [also published in *Die Kunst* 6 (1902)].

"Die moderne Umbildung unserer ästhetischen Anschauungen." *Deutsche Monatsschrift für das gesamte Leben der Gegenwart* 1 (1902): 686–702.

"Preface." In *Baillie Scott, London: Haus eines Kunst-Freundes.* Vol. 1 of *Meister der Innenkunst.* Darmstadt: Alex Koch, [1902].

"Preface." In *Charles Rennie Mackintosh, Glasgow: Haus eines Kunstfreundes.* Vol. 2 of *Meister der Innenkunst.* Darmstadt: Alex Koch, [1902].

"Preisschrift für die Anlage einer Heilstätte für Lungenkranke in England." *Centralblatt der Bauverwaltung* 22 (1902): 96.

Stilarchitektur und Baukunst: Wandlungen der Architektur im xix. Jahrhundert und ihr heutiger Standpunkt. Mülheim an der Ruhr: K. Schimmelpfeng, 1902.

"Die 'Wiederherstellung' von Baudenkmälern." *Neue Deutsche Rundschau* 13 (1902): 156–68.

"Zur Rettung unserer alten Bauten." *Dekorative Kunst* 5 (1902): 264–68 [also published in *Die Kunst* 6 (1902)].

1903

"Alte Volkstradition und modernes Parvenutum in unserer Baukunst." *Deutsche Monatsschrift für das gesamte Leben der Gegenwart* 3 (1903): 219–24.

"Englisches Mobiliar und M. H. Baillie Scott." *Innendekoration* 14, no. 7 (1903): 165–74.

"Das gesunde Haus." *Zentralblatt der Bauverwaltung* 23 (1903): 164 [review of Otto Kröhnke and H. Müllenbach. *Das gesunde Haus.* Stuttgart: Ferdinand Enke, 1902].

"Das japanische Haus." *Zentralblatt der Bauverwaltung* 23 (1903): 306–7 [review of Franz Baltzer. *Das japanische Haus.* Berlin: Wilhelm Ernst & Sohn, 1903].

"Die Kodak-Läden George Walton's." *Dekorative Kunst* 6 (1903): 201–13 [also published in *Die Kunst* 8 (1903)].

"Landhäuser der Architekten J. W. Bedford und S. D. Kitson in Leeds." *Dekorative Kunst* 6
(1903): 81–97 [also published in *Die Kunst* 8 (1903)].

"Sachliche Kunst: Kunstgewerbe, Jugendstil und bürgerliche Kunst." *Die Rheinlande* 4 (1903):
53–61.

*Stilarchitektur und Baukunst: Wandlungen der Architektur und der gewerblichen Künste im 19.
Jahrhundert und ihr heutiger Standpunkt.* 2nd ed., rev. and exp. Mülheim an der Ruhr:
K. Schimmelpfeng, 1903.

"Turin 1902." *Zentralblatt der Bauverwaltung* 23 (1903): 88 [review of Leo Nacht. *Turin 1902.*
Berlin: Ernst Wasmuth, 1902].

1904

"Amerika." *Der Kunstwart* 18, part 1, no. 5 (1904): 345–56.

"Auf dem VI. internationalen Architektenkongreß in Madrid." *Die Denkmalpflege* 6 (1904): 52.

"Die Bedeutung und gesetzgeberische Behandlung des Verkehrs mit Straßenlokomotiven in
England." *Zentralblatt der Bauverwaltung* 24 (1904): 313–15, 318–19.

Das englische Haus: Entwicklung, Bedingungen, Anlage, Aufbau, Einrichtung und Innenraum. 3
vols. Berlin: Ernst Wasmuth, 1904–1905.

"Das englische Haus und die nationale Bedeutung des Einzelhauses." *Deutsche Monatsschrift
für das gesamte Leben der Gegenwart* 5 (1904): 212–21.

"Das englische Haus und seine Räume." *Berliner Tageblatt* (25 January 1904): Beiblatt no. 4,
"Der Zeitgeist."

"Kultur und Kunst: Betrachtungen über das deutsche Kunstgewerbe." *Deutsche Monatsschrift
für das gesamte Leben der Gegenwart* 6 (1904): 72–87.

Kultur und Kunst: Gesammelte Aufsätze über künstlerische Fragen der Gegenwart. Jena: Eugen
Diederichs, 1904 [collection of previously published essays].

"'Kunst' im Gewerbe." *Der Kunstwart* 17, part 1, no. 9 (1904): 530–35.

"Die Kunst Richard Riemerschmids." *Dekorative Kunst* 7 (1904): 249–83 [also published in
Die Kunst 10 (1904)].

Das moderne Landhaus und seine innere Ausstattung. Munich: F. Bruckmann, 1904.

"Der VI. internationale Architekten-Kongreß in Madrid vom 6. bis 13. April 1904." *Zentralblatt
der Bauverwaltung* 24 (1904): 225–27.

"Das sogenannte Moderne in der Architektur der Neuzeit." *Der Baumeister* 2 (1904): 79–81.

"Über das Moderne in der Architektur." *Zentralblatt der Bauverwaltung* 24 (1904): 236–37.

"Über häusliche Baukunst." *Deutsche Bauhütte* 8, no. 31 (1904): 205–6.

"Unsere Kunstzustände: Ausdruck unserer Kultur." *Der Kunstwart* 17, part 2, no. 23 (1904):
464–73.

Die Wohnungs-Kunst auf der Welt-Ausstellung in St. Louis 1904. Darmstadt: Alexander Koch,
1904 [first published in *Deutsche Kunst und Dekoration* 15 (1904): 209–27].

1905

"Alfred Waterhouse †." *Zentralblatt der Bauverwaltung* 25 (1905): 459.

"Die Anfänge der modernen Innenkunst." *Die neue Rundschau* 16, part 2 (1905): 1025–50.

"Die Anlage des modernen Landhauses." *Die Werkkunst* 1 (1905): 25–27.

"Der Englische Garten." *Die neue Rundschau* 16, part 1 (1905): 428–35.

"Das englische Haus der Gegenwart." *Der Baumeister* 3 (1905): 6–9.

"Die Entwicklung des künstlerischen Gedankens im Hausbau." *Die Rheinlande* 5 (1905): 257–65.

"Hochbaulexikon." *Zentralblatt der Bauverwaltung* 25 (1905): 144 [review of Gustav Schönermark and Wilhelm Stüber, eds. *Hochbaulexicon*. Berlin: Wilhelm Ernst & Sohn, 1902–1904].

"Das moderne Landhaus." *Zentralblatt der Bauverwaltung* 25 (1905): 100 [review of Joseph August Lux. *Das moderne Landhaus*. Vienna: Anton Schroll, 1903].

Das moderne Landhaus und seine innere Ausstattung. 2nd ed., rev. and exp. Munich: F. Bruckmann, 1905.

"Der Weg und das Endziel des Kunstgewerbes." *Dekorative Kunst* 8 (1905): 181–90, 230–38 [also published in *Die Kunst* 12 (1905)].

Wohnungskultur. Dürerbund: Flugschrift zur ästhetischen Kultur, vol. 3. Munich: G. D. W. Callwey, 1905.

"Zur kunstgewerblichen Lage." *Die Werkkunst* 1 (1905): 4–7.

1906

Die Anlage des Landhauses. Dürerbund: Flugschrift zur ästhetischen Kultur, vol. 11. Munich: G. D. W. Callwey, 1906.

"Die Bedeutung der 3. Deutschen Kunstgewerbe-Ausstellung." In *3. Deutsche Kunstgewerbe-Ausstellung Dresden 1906.* Ausstellungs-Zeitung, no. 1 (1906): 2ff.

"Echtfärberei." *Die Werkkunst* 2 (1906): 3–4 [also published in both *Dekorative Kunst* 10 (1907): 335–36 and *Hohe Warte* 3, part 11 (1907): 183].

"The Education of the Public in Architecture." *Journal of the Royal Institute of British Architects* 13, 3rd ser. (1906): XLII–XLIII [summary of the proceedings of the VIIth International Congress of Architects, London, 16–21 July 1906].

"Die Entwicklung des künstlerischen Gedankens im Hausbau." In *Die künstlerische Gestaltung des Arbeiter-Wohnhauses*, 7–15. Schriften der Centralstelle für Arbeiter- und Wohlfahrtseinrichtungen, no. 29. Berlin: Carl Henmann, 1906.

"Ein Erfolg des deutschen Kunstgewerbes." *Die Werkkunst* 1 (1906): 305–8.

"Die Erziehung zur Architektur." *Der Kunstwart* 20, part 1, no. 4 (1906): 191–93.

"Geschichtliche Entwicklung des Kunstunterrichts im XVIII. Jahrhundert." *Hohe Warte* 2, part 12 (1906): 158–59.

"Das Kunstgewerbe." *Die Weltwirtschaft* 1, part 1 (1906): 312–25.

"Kunstgewerbliche Erziehung und Zeichenunterricht." In *Sammlung der Drucksachen des . Preußischen Hauses der Abgeordneten*, 99–143. Anlagen zu den Stenographischen Berichten 6, no. 257 (Berlin, 1906).

"Das Maschinenmöbel." *Hohe Warte* 2, part 1 (1906): 2 [also published in *Fachblatt für Holzarbeiter* 1 (1906)].

"Der moderne Ziegelbau in England unter Vorführung von Lichtbildern." *Tonindustrie-Zeitung* 30, no. 61 (1906): 928–38.

"Die neuere Entwicklung des kunstgewerblichen Gedankens." *Der Sämann* 2 (1906): 200–205.

"Die neuere Entwicklung und der heutige Stand des kunstgewerblichen Schulwesens in Preußen." In *Das Deutsche Kunstgewerbe 1906: III. Deutsche Kunstgewerbe-Ausstellung Dresden 1906*, 41–51. Munich: F. Bruckmann, 1906.

"Der siebente internationale Architektenkongreß in London." *Zentralblatt der Bauverwaltung* 26 (1906): 398–400, 403.

"Sommer- und Ferienhäuser: Eine Anregung zu einem Preisausschreiben." *Die Woche* 8, no. 36 (8 September 1906): 1545–46.

"Vom falschen Scheine." *Die Werkkunst* 1 (1906): 249–50.

1907

"Architektur und Publikum." *Die neue Rundschau* 18, part 1 (1907): 204–14.

"Die Bedeutung des Kunstgewerbes." *Hohe Warte* 3, part 15 (1907): 233–38.

"Die Bedeutung des Kunstgewerbes: Eröffnungsrede zu den Vorlesungen über modernes Kunstgewerbe an der Handelshochschule in Berlin." *Dekorative Kunst* 10 (1907): 177–92 [also published in *Die Kunst* 16 (1907)].

"Das Bundesziel." *Hohe Warte* 3, part 19 (1907): 297.

"Die Entstehungsgeschichte und Bedeutung der Wiener Kunstgewerbeschule." *Die Werkkunst* 3 (1907): 201–2.

"Erziehung zur Architektur." *Bautechnische Zeitschrift* 22, no. 19 (1907): 147–49.

"Gutachten über das Programm der Lehrwerkstätten der 'Deutschen Werkstätten für Handwerkskunst.'" *Hohe Warte* 3, part 20 (1907): 322–23.

"Kunstgewerbe und Architektur." *Hohe Warte* 3, part 12 (1907): 185–86.

Kunstgewerbe und Architektur. Jena: Eugen Diederichs, 1907 [collection of previously published essays].

"Kunstgewerbe- und Handwerkerschulen." In *Bücher- und Lehrmittelschau nichtamtliche Beilage des Landesgewerbeamts zum Ministerial-Blatt der Handels- und Gewerbe-Verwaltung* 1 (1907): 74ff.

Landhaus und Garten: Beispiele neuzeitlicher Landhäuser nebst Grundrissen, Innenräumen und Gärten. Munich: F. Bruckmann, 1907.

"M. H. Baillie Scott-Bedford." *Deutsche Kunst und Dekoration* 19 (1907): 423–31.

"Das Moderne in der Architektur." *Die Werkkunst* 3 (1907): 326–29.

"Die nationale Bedeutung der kunstgewerblichen Bewegung." *Die Rheinlande* 7 (March 1907):
    22–33 [also published in *Hohe Warte* 3, part 1 (1907): 16].

"Pflege alter Marktplätze." *Die Rheinlande* 7 (July 1907): 21.

"Probleme des Kunstgewerbes." *Die Werkkunst* 3 (1907): 25–29.

"Sommer- und Ferienhäuser." In *Sommer- und Ferienhäuser aus dem Wettbewerb der Woche*,
    VII–X. Sonderhefte der Woche, vol. 10. Berlin: August Scherl, 1907.

"Der Weg und das Ziel des Kunstgewerbes." *Fachblatt für Holzarbeiter* 2 (1907): 65ff., 85ff.

"Zu unserm Preisausschreiben: Entwürfe für Sommer- und Ferienhäuser." *Die Woche* 9, no. 7
    (16 February 1907): 267–68, 270.

"Zur Denkmalspflege." *Die Rheinlande* 7 (April 1907): 120.

1908

"Die Architektur auf den Ausstellungen in Darmstadt, München und Wien." *Kunst und Künst-
    ler* 6 (1908): 491–95.

"Der Deutsche Werkbund." *Die Zeit* [Vienna] 7, no. 2115 (1908).

Die Einheit der Architektur: Betrachtungen über Baukunst, Ingenieurbau und Kunstgewerbe. Ber-
    lin: Karl Curtius, 1908 [speech given at the Verein für Kunst, Berlin, on 13 February
    1908].

Das englische Haus: Entwicklung, Bedingungen, Anlage, Aufbau, Einrichtung und Innenraum. 3
    vols. 2nd ed., rev. Berlin: Ernst Wasmuth, 1908–1911.

"Das englische Haus." *Die Woche* 10, no. 25 (1908): 1057–59.

"Das Hausbauproblem und die Häuserausstellung der 'Woche' in Neu-Finkenkrug und Wand-
    litzsee." *Neudeutsche Bauzeitung* 4 (1908): 267–69.

"Hygiene und Wohnungskunst." *Unser Hausarzt* (1908): 140–41.

"Kunst und Volkswirtschaft." *Dokumente des Fortschritts* 1, no. 2 (January 1908): 115–20.

"Kunstgewerbe und Leben: Der Deutsche Werkbund." *Allgemeine Zeitung* [Munich] (11 July
    1908): 296–98.

"Die Lage des Landhauses zur Sonne und zum Garten." *Der Baumeister* 6 (1908): 1–6, 19–23.

"Landhaus in der Parkstraße 56, Dahlem." *Der Baumeister* 6 (1908): 6–8.

"Mein Haus in Nikolassee." *Deutsche Kunst und Dekoration* 23 (1908): 1–21.

"Das Moderne in der Architektur." In Johannes Mumbauer, ed. *Trierisches Jahrbuch für ästhe-
    tische Kultur*, 78–83. Trier: n.p., 1908.

"Das Musikzimmer." In *Almanach*, 222–37. Berlin: Velhagen & Klasing, 1908.

"Die neue Architektur." *Bautechnische Zeitschrift* 23 (1908): 273–76.

Die Veredelung der gewerblichen Arbeit im Zusammenwirken von Kunst, Industrie und Handwerk,
    37–53, 143–50. Verhandlung des Deutschen Werkbundes zu München am 11. und 12.

Juli 1908. Leipzig: R. Voigtländer, 1908 [speech given at the Deutscher Werkbund, Munich, in July 1908].

"Des Werkbundes Ziele." *Die Zeit* [Vienna] 7, no. 2123 (1908).

"Wirtschaftsformen im Kunstgewerbe." *Die Werkkunst* 3 (1908): 230–31.

"Wirtschaftsformen im Kunstgewerbe." *Volkswirtschaftliche Zeitfragen* 30, no. 1 (1908): 3–31 [speech given at the Volkswirtschaftliche Gesellschaft, Berlin, on 30 January 1908].

1909

"Die ästhetische Ausbildung unserer Ingenieurbauten." *Zeitschrift des Vereines deutscher Ingenieure* 53 (1909): 1211–17 [address given at the fiftieth congress of the Verein deutscher Ingenieure, Wiesbaden, 1909].

"Einfache schweizerische Wohnhäuser." *Neudeutsche Bauzeitung* 5, no. 4 (1909): 39–43.

Kultur und Kunst. 2nd ed. Jena: Eugen Diederichs, 1909.

"Zur architektonischen Lage." *Neudeutsche Bauzeitung* 5, no. 1 (1909): 1–5.

1910

"Die Ausstellung für Kunsthandwerk und Kunstindustrie in Stockholm 1909." *Kunstgewerbeblatt*, n.s., 21 (1910): 22–26.

"Eindrücke von der Brüssler Welt-Ausstellung." *Deutsche Kunst und Dekoration* 27 (1910): 33–37.

Landhaus und Garten: Beispiele neuzeitlicher Landhäuser nebst Grundrissen, Innenräumen und Gärten. 2nd ed., rev. and exp. Munich: F. Bruckmann, 1910.

"Das Moderne in der Architektur." *Süddeutsche Bauzeitung* 20 (1910): 419–24.

"Städtebau." *Kunst und Künstler* 8 (1910): 531–35.

"Die Stellung der Kunst in der Volkswirtschaft." *Volkswirtschaftliche Blätter* 9, no. 15/16 (1910): 260–64 [speech given at the Volkswirtschaftliche Verbande].

1911

"Architectur." *Über Land und Meer* 105 (1911): 94–95, 320–21, 421–22, 515–16, 613–14.

"Architectur." *Über Land und Meer* 106 (1911): 719–21, 821–22, 934, 1039–40, 1136, 1225–26, 1317–18.

"Die Bedeutung der Kunst für das sittliche und wirtschaftliche Leben." *Neudeutsche Bauzeitung* 7 (1911): 247–49.

"Die Bedeutung des architektonischen Formgefühls für die Kultur unserer Zeit: Vortrag, gehalten auf der Jahresversammlung des Deutschen Werkbundes in Dresden 1911." *Architektonische Rundschau* 27 (1911): 121–25, 133–39.

"Das deutsche Kunstgewerbe in Brüssel." *Kunst und Künstler* 9 (1911): 54–57.

"Landhäuser." *Dekorative Kunst* 14 (1911): 1–24 [also published in *Die Kunst* 24 (1911)].

"Reaktion im Kunstgewerbe." *Die Zeit* [Vienna] 10, no. 3188 (1911).

1912

Dernburg, Bernhard, Alexander Dominicus, Hermann Muthesius, and Albert Südekum. *Was erwarten wir vom Zweckverband?* Vol. 1 of *Für Groß-Berlin*. Charlottenburg: Vita, 1912.

Dessoir, Max, and Hermann Muthesius. *Das Bismarck-Nationaldenkmal: Eine Erörterung des Wettbewerbes*. Jena: Eugen Diederichs, 1912.

"Alfred Messel." *Die Gartenlaube*, no. 11 (1912): 226–30.

"Die Anlage des Landhauses." *Die Bauwelt* 3, no. 10 (1912): 11–13.

"Architectur." *Über Land und Meer* 107 (1912): 86–87, 197, 323, 424–25, 449, 528–29, 634–35.

"Architectur." *Über Land und Meer* 108 (1912): 140–41, 250–51, 364–65, 466–67, 564–65, 656–58, 704–705.

"Die deutsche Architektur der Zukunft." In Emil Abigt, ed. *Landhaus und Villa*, 161–66. Wiesbaden: Westdeutsche Verlagsgesellschaft, 1912.

"Komfort, Hygiene und fließendes Wasser in Schlafzimmern." *Die Bauwelt* 3, no. 20 (1912): 13–14.

Landhäuser. Munich: F. Bruckmann, 1912.

"Die Wirtschafts- und Nebenräume des Hauses." In Emil Abigt, ed. *Landhaus und Villa*, 323–48. Wiesbaden: Westdeutsche Verlagsgesellschaft, 1912.

"Wo stehen wir?" In *Die Durchgeistigung der Deutschen Arbeit: Wege und Ziele in Zusammenhang von Industrie, Handwerk und Kunst*, 11–26. Jena: Eugen Diederichs, 1912 [speech given at the fourth annual meeting of the Deutscher Werkbund, Dresden, 1911].

1913

"Architectur." *Über Land und Meer* 109 (1913): 88, 196–97, 318–19, 422–23, 526–27, 546–48, 629–30.

"Architectur." *Über Land und Meer* 110 (1913): 736–37, 844–45, 949–50, 1084–85, 1182–83, 1274–75, 1367–68.

"Architektur, Kunstgewerbe, Landschaft." In *Das Jahr 1913*, 495–503. Leipzig: B. G. Teubner, 1913.

"Die deutsche Architektur der Gegenwart." *Illustrierte Zeitung* 140, no. 3647 (22 May 1913): 17–18.

"Das Formproblem im Ingenieurbau." In *Die Kunst in Industrie und Handel*, 23–32. Jahrbuch des Deutschen Werkbundes. Jena: Eugen Diederichs, 1913 [also published in *Schweizerische Bauzeitung* 62 (1913): 31–32, 99–101, 129–30].

"Der moderne Stil." *Arena*, part 3 (1913–1914): 1811ff.

"Die neuere architektonische Bewegung in Deutschland." *Dokumente des Fortschritts* 6, no. 3 (March 1913): 183–88.

"Sanitäre Anlagen im Hause." *Dekorative Kunst* 16 (1913): 328 [also published in *Die Kunst* 28 (1913)].

"Sinn und Ziel der Bauberatung." *Die Bauwelt* 4, no. 3 (16 January 1913): Beilage, "Die Bauberatung," 23–27.

"Was unseren Universitäten fehlt." *Berliner Illustrierte Zeitung* 22 (1913): 517–19.

"Der Zug der Unrast." *Dekorative Kunst* 16 (1913): 283 [also published in *Die Kunst* 28 (1913)].

"Zweck und Schönheit." *Der Kunstfreund* 1, no. 2 (1913): 33–37.

1914

"Architectur." *Über Land und Meer* 111 (1914): 82–83, 189–90, 308–9, 412–13, 508–10, 578–79.

"Architectur." *Über Land und Meer* 112 (1914): 701–2, 808–10, 914, 1024–25, 1125–26, 1223–24.

"Ein Baudenkmal." *Bau-Rundschau* 10 (1914): 86–87.

Die Bedeutung der Gartenstadtbewegung. Deutsche Gartenstadt-Gesellschaft. Leipzig: R. Federn, 1914 [collection of speeches given in the presence of the crown princess].

"Haus Huffmann in Cottbus." *Dekorative Kunst* 17 (1914): 505–12 [also published in *Die Kunst* 30 (1914)].

"Krieg und Kultur." *Illustrierte Zeitung* 143, no. 3718 (1 October 1914): 507–10.

"Vom Kunstgewerbe zum Werkbundgedanken." *Illustrierte Zeitung*, Werkbund Nummer 142, no. 3699 (21 May 1914): 2–6.

"Was will der Deutsche Werkbund?" *Die Woche* 16, no. 23 (1914): 969–72.

"Die Werkbund-Arbeit der Zukunft." In *Hermann Muthesius Die Werkbund-Arbeit der Zukunft. . . . Der Werkbund-Gedanke in den germanischen Ländern.* Jena: Eugen Diederichs, 1914.

"Zweck und Ziel des deutschen Werkbundes." *Berliner Tageblatt* (28 May 1914): 11.

1915

"Architectur." *Über Land und Meer* 113 (1915): 165.

" 'Deutsche Mode.' " *Der Kunstwart* 28, no. 12 (1915): 205–8.

Der Deutsche nach dem Kriege. Weltkultur und Weltpolitik, Deutsche Folge, vol. 4. Edited by Ernst Jäckh. Munich: F. Bruckmann, 1915.

"Das Geschmeide der reichen Leute." *Vossische Zeitung*, no. 260 (1915): Beilage 5.

"Haus Dryander in Zabitz." *Dekorative Kunst* 18 (1915): 41–47 [also published in *Die Kunst* 32 (1915)].

"Kommende Krieger-Denkmäler." *Vossische Zeitung*, no. 608 (28 November 1915): Beilage 4.

"Der Krieg und die deutsche Modeindustrie." *Die Woche* 17, no. 11 (1915): 363–65.

"Wohnungsbau in Einheitsformen, Stimmen zu dem Aufsatz in Heft 4." *Der Baumeister* 13 (1915): 62.

Die Zukunft der deutschen Form. Der Deutsche Krieg: Politische Flugschriften, vol. 50. Edited by Ernst Jäckh. Stuttgart and Berlin: Deutsche Verlags-Anstalt, 1915.

"Zum Wiederaufbau Ostpreußens." *Der Tag*, no. 180 (4 August 1915): Ausgabe B.

"Zur Nagelung von Wahrzeichen." *Der Tag*, no. 224 (24 September 1915): Ausgabe A.

1916

"Deutsches Bauschaffen nach dem Kriege." *Wasmuths Monatshefte für Baukunst* 2 (1915/1916): 189–93, 309–15.

"Deutsches Hausgerät." *Wieland* 1, nos. 42–44 (January 1916): 10–11.

Deutsches Kunstgewerbe und Bauschaffen nach dem Kriege. Berlin: Ernst Wasmuth, 1916 [speech given at the Verein für Deutsches Kunstgewerbes, Berlin, on 2 February 1916. First published in *Wasmuths Monatshefte für Baukunst* 2 (1915/1916)].

"England und das deutsche Kunstgewerbe." *Die Woche* 18, no. 13 (1916): 433–35.

"Heimatkunst und Einheitsform: Aus einem Vortrage über den Wiederaufbau kriegszerstörter Ortschaften." *Dekorative Kunst* 19 (1916): 159–65 [also published in *Die Kunst* 34 (1916)].

"Kommende Krieger-Denkmäler." *Die Rheinlande* 16, no. 5 (1916): 177–79.

"Die mechanische Seidenweberei Michels & Cie. in Nowawes bei Potsdam." *Dekorative Kunst* 19 (1916): 190–94 [also published in *Die Kunst* 34 (1916)].

"Ostpreußen und sein Wiederaufbau." *Wieland* 2, no. 5 (August 1916): 14–15.

"Die Werkbundarbeit der Handlungsgehilfen." *Jahrbuch für deutschnationale Handlungsgehilfen* 17 (1916): 97–99.

"Der Werkbundgedanke: Seine Grundlagen." *Deutsche Politik: Wochenschrift für Welt- und Kulturpolitik* 1, no. 10 (1916): 459–67.

1917

"Bemerkungen zur Erziehung der zeichnerischen Hilfskräfte in Architektur und Kunstgewerbe." *Wieland* 3, no. 1 (April 1917): 17–18.

Handarbeit und Massenerzeugnis. Technische Abende im Zentralinstitut für Erziehung und Unterricht, vol. 4. Berlin: E. S. Mittler, 1917.

"Haus Wegmann in Rhede (Bez. Münster)." *Dekorative Kunst* 20 (1917): 113–18 [also published in *Die Kunst* 36 (1917)].

"Kommende Krieger-Denkmäler." *Christliches Kunstblatt für Kirche, Schule und Haus* 49 (1917): 183–86.

"Wie baue ich mein Haus?" *Dekorative Kunst* 20 (1917): 282–87 [also published in *Die Kunst* 36 (1917)].

Wie baue ich mein Haus? Munich: F. Bruckmann, 1917.

Wie baue ich mein Haus? 2nd ed., rev. and exp. Munich: F. Bruckmann, 1917.

"Wie wird der Krieg auf die deutsche Baukunst einwirken?" *Deutsche Kunst und Dekoration* 40 (1917): 178–80 [also published in *Der unsichtbare Tempel: Monatsschrift zur Sammlung der Geister* 2, no. 5 (1917) and *Zeit- und Streitfragen: Korrespondenz des Bundes deutscher Gelehrter und Künstler*, no. 9 (9 March 1917)].

1918

"Das deutsche Haus von Paul Ehmig." *Wasmuths Monatshefte für Baukunst* 3 (1918): 128–30.

"Das deutsche Kunstgewerbe." In Georg Gellert, ed. *Das deutsche Buch fürs deutsche Volk*, 304–11. Berlin: Phönix, 1918.

"Kleinhaus und Kleinsiedlung." *Verkehrstechnische Woche und eisenbahntechnische Zeitschrift* 12, no. 14/17 (1918): 49–58 [speech given at the Verein für Eisenbahnkunde, Berlin, on 13 November 1917].

Kleinhaus und Kleinsiedlung. Munich: F. Bruckmann, 1918.

"Maßnahmen zur Bekämpfung der Wohnungsnot in der Übergangszeit." *Dekorative Kunst* 21 (1918): 87–92 [also published in *Die Kunst* 38 (1918)].

"Soll die kunstgewerbliche Erziehung zukünftig den Akademien übertragen werden?" *Die Woche* 20, no. 20 (1918): 489–91.

"Der Verkehr als Kulturförderer." In *Bericht über die XVII. Ordentliche Hauptversammlung vom 20. bis 22. September 1918 in Weimar*, 56–71. Veröffentlichungen des Bundes Deutscher Verkehrs-Vereine, no. 9. Leipzig: Deutsche Verkehrs-Vereine, 1918.

"Die Verpflichtung zur Form." *Dekorative Kunst* 21 (1918): 305–16 [also published in *Die Kunst* 38 (1918)].

"Vom Äußeren des Hauses." *Dekorative Kunst* 21 (1918): 10–11 [also published in *Die Kunst* 38 (1918)].

"Zwei Bauten von Hermann Muthesius." *Dekorative Kunst* 21 (1918): 105–20 [also published in *Die Kunst* 38 (1918)].

1919

Eberstadt, Rudolf, and Hermann Muthesius. "Kleinsiedelung der Hermsdorfer Bodengesellschaft in Hermsdorf bei Berlin." *Der Städtebau* 16 (1919): 6–9.

"Architektonisches über die Großstation Nauen." *Telefunken-Zeitung* 3, no. 17 (1919): 32–45.

"Bebauungsplan für die Kleinsiedlung Tannenwalde bei Königsberg." *Wasmuths Monatshefte für Baukunst* 4, no. 5/6 (1919): 152–60.

"Fritz Schumachers Bautätigkeit in Hamburg." *Dekorative Kunst* 22 (1919): 93–110 [also published in *Die Kunst* 40 (1919)].

"Die Häuser Rümelin in Heilbronn und Cramer in Dahlem." *Dekorative Kunst* 22 (1919): 1–16 [also published in *Die Kunst* 40 (1919)].

"Heimatkunst und Einheitsform." *Die Heimatkunst* 1, no. 3 (1919): 73–79.

Landhaus und Garten: Beispiele kleinerer Landhäuser nebst Grundrissen, Innenräumen und Gärten. 3rd ed., rev. Munich: F. Bruckmann, 1919.

"Der Mittelhof in Nikolassee." *Dekorative Kunst* 22 (1919): 281–89 [also published in *Die Kunst* 40 (1919)].

"Die Möblierung des Kleinhauses." *Das Tischlergewerk* 12, no. 8 (1919): 65–68 [first published in *Mitteilungen des Bundes der Kunstgewerbeschulmänner*, no. 3 (1918): 1–4].

"Vom Garten des Kleinhauses." *Dekorative Kunst* 22 (1919): 240–46 [also published in *Die Kunst* 40 (1919)].

Wie baue ich mein Haus? 3rd ed., rev. Munich: F. Bruckmann, 1919.

"Zwei Siedlungsbauten in 'Ibus'-Bauweise: 1. Das Arbeiter-Doppelhaus." *Sitzungsberichte des Arbeitsausschusses im Reichsverband zur Förderung sparsamer Bauweise* 1, no. 1 (1919): 28–31.

1920

"Aufbau vom Kunstgewerbe her." *Propyläen* 17 (1920): 126.

"Die Baukunst im Dienste der kaufmännischen Werbetätigkeit." *Das Plakat* 11, no. 6 (1920): 259–68.

"Der geordnete Garten." *Stadtbaukunst alter und neuer Zeit* 21 (1920): 337–39; 22 (1920): 358–61.

"Die geschmackliche Verbesserung des Massenerzeugnisses." *Deutsche Industrie* 1, no. 31 (1920): 591ff.

Kann ich auch jetzt noch mein Haus bauen? Richtlinien für den wirklich sparsamen Bau des bürgerlichen Einfamilienhauses unter den wirtschaftlichen Beschränkungen der Gegenwart. Munich: F. Bruckmann, 1920.

Kleinhaus und Kleinsiedlung. 2nd ed., rev. and exp. Munich: F. Bruckmann, 1920.

"'Kleinwohnungen' und 'Luxuswohnungen.'" *Berliner Tageblatt*, no. 581 (1920): Beiblatt 4.

"Die Mustermesse als Geschmackserzieherin." *Kunst und Industrie* 1 (1920): 51–53.

"Qualitätsarbeit und Luxusbekämpfung." *Berliner Tageblatt*, no. 500 (1920): Beiblatt 4.

"Vereinfachung der Inneneinrichtung." *Hausrat* 1 (1920): 76–78.

1921

"Architektonisches über die Großstation Nauen." *Der Industriebau* 12 (1921): 43ff.

"Die Lage im Wohnungsbau." *Kultur-Korrespondenz für deutsche Zeitungen des In- und Auslandes* 6, no. 24 (1921).

"Die notwendigen und entbehrlichen Räume des Hauses." *Dekorative Kunst* 24 (1921): 110–12, 116–20 [also published in *Die Kunst* 44 (1918)].

"Die Qualität, ein Leitsatz der deutschen Industrie der Zukunft." *Zeiss-Werkzeitung* 2, no. 4 (1921): 62ff.

"Über Architektur und Architekten-Erziehung." *Die Baugilde* 3, no. 16 (1921).

"Was wird aus den Kunstgewerbeschulen?" *Berliner Tageblatt*, no. 203 (1920): Beiblatt 1.

"Zur Architektur der Großfunkenstation Nauen." *Schweizerische Bauzeitung* 77, no. 13 (1921): 142–45.

1922

"Die Kunstgewerbe- und Handwerkerschule." In *Kunstgewerbe: Ein Bericht über Entwicklung und Tätigkeit der Handwerker- und Kunstgewerbeschulen in Preußen*, 1–10. Berlin: Ernst Wasmuth, 1922.

Landhäuser: Ausgeführte Bauten mit Grundrissen, Gartenplänen und Erläuterungen. 2nd ed., exp. Munich: F. Bruckmann, 1922.

"Rückkehr zum Handwerk?" *Nürnberger Warte: Zeitschrift des Großeinkaufsverbandes 'Nürnberger Bund'* 2 (1922): Beilage, "Kunst und Kunstgewerbe," 1ff.

Die schöne Wohnung: Beispiele neuer deutscher Innenräume. Munich: F. Bruckmann, 1922.

"Seidenweberei Michels in Nowawes." *Neudeutsche Bauzeitung* 18 (1922): 189–90.

"Sparsamkeit und gute Form im künftigen Wohnungsbau." *Deutschland: Zeitschrift für Aufbau*, part 4 (1922): 70.

"Über den Individualismus in der Architektur." *Schweizerische Bauzeitung* 80, no. 11 (1922): 123–26.

1923

"Der japanische Hausbau." *Berliner Tageblatt*, no. 429 (1923): Beiblatt 1.

"Die kommenden Aufgaben der Berufsschule: Ein neuer Bildungsgedanke." *Leipziger Tageblatt und Handelszeitung*, no. 164 (1923): 4.

"Landschaft und Menschenwerk." *Berliner Tageblatt*, no. 234 (1923): Beiblatt 4.

"Das verkleinerte Landhaus." *Schweizerische Bauzeitung* 81, no. 16 (1923): 194–98.

"Vom Bauen nach dem Kriege." *Berliner Tageblatt*, no. 217 (1923): Beiblatt 1.

"Das zu große Haus." *Dekorative Kunst* 26 (1923): 210–22 [also published in *Die Kunst* 48 (1923)].

1924

"Die Bautätigkeit in Deutschland." In Robert Kuczynski, ed. *Deutschland und Frankreich: Ihre Wirtschaft und ihre Politik 1923/24*, 290–96. Berlin: R. L. Prager, 1924.

"Deutschland auf der Kunstausstellung in Paris: Die notwendigen Vorbereitungen." *Berliner Tageblatt,* no. 557 (1924): Beiblatt 1.

"Die Siedlung der Zukunft." *Dekorative Kunst* 27 (1924): 38–42 [also published in *Die Kunst* 50 (1923)].

"Die Suggestion der Form." *Dekorative Kunst* 27 (1924): 94–96 [also published in *Die Kunst* 50 (1923)].

"Die Wiederbelebung der Bautätigkeit." *Deutsche Handelswarte*, no. 5/6 (1924): 97–102; no. 7 (1924): 135–40.

"Zeitfragen der Baukunst." *Ingenieur-Zeitschrift* 4, no. 4 (1924): 245–49.

"Zur Wiederbelebung der Bautätigkeit." *Bauamt und Gemeindebau*, no. 10 (1924): 95–96.

1925

"Die Erziehung des baukünstlerischen Nachwuchses." *Deutsche Bauzeitung* 59, no. 35 (1925): 277–78; no. 38 (1925): 298–300 [also published in *Zentralblatt der Bauverwaltung* 45 (1925): 190].

"Die Evolution des Kunstgewerbes in Deutschland." In Robert Kuczynski, ed. *Deutschland und Frankreich: Ihre Wirtschaft und ihre Politik 1923/24*, 9–11. Berlin: R. L. Prager, 1925.

"Exportfragen." *Mitteilungen des deutschen Werkbundes*, no. 1 (1925): 1ff.

"Hauptforderungen der Kunsterziehung." *Berliner Tageblatt*, no. 120 (1925): Beiblatt 1.

"Haus T. in Berlin-Charlottenburg." *Die Bauwelt* 16, no. 9 (1925): 181–86.

"Hauszinssteuerbauten: Der Mangel an Bequemlichkeit und Wohnlichkeit." *Berliner Tageblatt*, no. 260 (1925): Beiblatt 1.

Landhaus und Garten: Beispiele neuzeitlicher Landhäuser nebst Grundrissen, Innenräumen und Gärten. 4th ed., rev. Munich: F. Bruckmann, 1925.

Wie baue ich mein Haus? Berufserfahrungen und Ratschläge eines Architekten. 4th ed., rev. Munich: F. Bruckmann, 1925.

1926

Die schöne Wohnung: Beispiele neuer deutscher Innenräume. 2nd ed., rev. Munich: F. Bruckmann, 1926.

"Werkbundausstellung oder Weltausstellung?" *Berliner Tageblatt*, no. 523 (1926).

Zur Frage der Erziehung des künstlerischen Nachwuchses. Berlin: Guido Hackebeil, 1926 [speech given at the Akademie des Bauwesens on 11 December 1925. First published in *Zentralblatt der Bauverwaltung* 46 (1926): 61–64, 75–77].

1927

"Der Kampf um das Dach." *Die Baugilde* 9 (1927): 191 [first published in *Deutsche Allgemeine Zeitung*, no. 48 (1926): Beilage, "Kraft und Stoff"].

"Kunst- und Modeströmungen." *Wasmuths Monatshefte für Baukunst* 11, no. 12 (1927): 496–98.

"Die letzten Worte eines Meisters: Die neue Bauweise." *Berliner Tageblatt*, no. 512 (1927): Beiblatt 1.

"Die neue Bauweise." *Die Baugilde* 9 (1927): 1284–86.

"Subventionierter Wohnungsbau." *Das ideale Heim* 1 (1927): 135–37.

1928

"Die neuere Entwicklung des kunstgewerblichen Gedankens und ihr Einfluß auf die Schulen."
Zeitschrift für Berufs- und Fachschulwesen 43, no. 1 (1928): 1–3.

"Die Ostdeutschen Werkstätten in Neiße." *Illustrierte Zeitung* 171, no. 4353 (1928): 242–44.

1933

"Der kombinierte Wohn-Eßraum im Eigenhause." *Das schöne Heim* 4, part 9 (1933): 275–79.

INDEX

STYLE-ARCHITECTURE AND BUILDING-ART:
TRANSFORMATIONS OF ARCHITECTURE
IN THE NINETEENTH CENTURY
AND ITS PRESENT CONDITION

Introduction and translation by Stanford Anderson

Stanford Anderson has written and lectured widely on the historiography of modern architecture and urbanism. His current projects include essays on the Deutsche Werkbund; a study contrasting the International Style with modern architecture in America and Scandinavia; an examination of new towns of the South Carolina Railroad; and an essay on Louis I. Kahn and public institutions. He is the head of the Department of Architecture at the Massachusetts Institute of Technology.

Designed by Lorraine Wild.
Composed by Wilsted & Taylor
in Berkeley Old Style Medium type (introduction),
Cloister Bold and Roman type (translation),
and Berkeley Old Style Book (heads and running heads).
Printed by Gardner Lithograph, Buena Park, California
on Mohawk Superfine 80 lb., white and off-white.
Bound by Roswell Book Bindery, Phoenix.

TEXTS & DOCUMENTS
Series designed by Laurie Haycock Makela and Lorraine Wild

TEXTS & DOCUMENTS
A SERIES OF THE GETTY CENTER PUBLICATION PROGRAMS

Julia Bloomfield, Thomas F. Reese, Salvatore Settis, *Editors*
Kurt W. Forster, *Consultative Editor*

Although Hermann Muthesius is best known today in Anglo-American architectural literature for his studies of the English house, these impressive volumes were only one aspect of a more encompassing modernist polemic emanating from the German realist movement of the late 1890s. *Style-Architecture and Building-Art*, published in 1902, was Muthesius's first serious effort to define the lineaments of early Modernism. A turn-of-the-century retrospective, it contains nearly all of the assumptions—good and bad—of later modernist historiography: the disdain of the nineteenth century for its artistic eclecticism and lack of originality; an appreciation of the material and industrial forces propelling the upheaval in building technologies; and, above all, a plea for a more *sachlich* (plain, simple) approach to design. This critical and highly opinionated text not only presages and underscores the tenets of the Deutsche Werkbund (founded five years later) but can itself be viewed as an important cornerstone of the Modern Movement.

IN PRINT

Otto Wagner, *Modern Architecture* (1902)
Introduction by Harry Francis Mallgrave
(Hardback, ISBN 0-226-86938-5. Paperback, ISBN 0-226-86939-3)

Heinrich Hübsch et al., *In What Style Should We Build? The German Debate on Architectural Style* (1828–1847)
Introduction by Wolfgang Herrmann
(Hardback, ISBN 0-89236-199-9. Paperback, ISBN 0-89236-198-0)

Nicolas Le Camus de Mézières, *The Genius of Architecture; or, The Analogy of That Art with Our Sensations* (1780)
Introduction by Robin Middleton
(Hardback, ISBN 0-89236-234-0. Paperback, ISBN 0-89236-235-9)

Claude Perrault, *Ordonnance for the Five Kinds of Columns after the Method of the Ancients* (1683)
Introduction by Alberto Pérez-Gómez
(Hardback, ISBN 0-89236-232-4. Paperback, ISBN 0-89236-233-2)

Robert Vischer, Conrad Fiedler, Heinrich Wölfflin, Adolf Göller, Adolf Hildebrand, and August Schmarsow, *Empathy, Form, and Space: Problems in German Aesthetics, 1873–1893*
Introduction by Harry Francis Mallgrave and Eleftherios Ikonomou
(Hardback, ISBN 0-89236-260-X. Paperback, ISBN 0-89236-259-6)

Friedrich Gilly: Essays on Architecture, 1796–1799
Introduction by Fritz Neumeyer
(Hardback, ISBN 0-89236-280-4. Paperback, ISBN 0-89236-281-2)

IN PREPARATION

Sigfried Giedion, *Building in France, Building in Iron, Building in Ferroconcrete* (1928)
Introduction by Sokratis Georgiadis

Hendrik Petrus Berlage, *Thoughts on Style* (1886–1911)
Introduction by Iain Boyd Whyte

All books in the TEXTS & DOCUMENTS series are distributed by the University of Chicago Press

LIBRARY OF CONGRESS CATALOGING-IN-PUBLICATION DATA

Muthesius, Hermann, 1861–1927.

   [Stilarchitektur und Baukunst. English]

   Style-architecture and building-art : transformations of architecture in the nineteenth century and its present condition / Hermann Muthesius ; introduction and translation by Stanford Anderson.

      p.   cm. — (Texts & documents)

   Translation of 1st ed., with indication of additions, deletions, and variations occurring in the 2nd ed.

   Includes bibliographical references and index.

   ISBN 0-89236-282-0. ISBN 0-89236-283-9 (pbk.).

   1. Architecture, Modern—19th century.   2. Modernism (Art)—Influence.   3. Architecture and society.   4. Architecture—Philosophy.   I. Title.   II. Series.

NA645.M8813   1994

724′.5—dc20   94-14964

                                                   CIP